WILL SUTTON

# GHOST TOWN

*Complete and Unabridged*

## LINFORD
*Leicester*

First published in Great Britain in 2000

First Linford Edition
published 2010

British Library CIP Data

Sutton, Will.
   Ghost town. - - (Linford western library)
   1. Western stories.
   2. Large type books.
   I. Title II. Series
   823.9'2–dc22

   ISBN 978–1–44480–168–2

Published by
F. A. Thorpe (Publishing)
Anstey, Leicestershire

Set by Words & Graphics Ltd.
Anstey, Leicestershire
Printed and bound in Great Britain by
T. J. International Ltd., Padstow, Cornwall

This book is printed on acid-free paper

# GHOST TOWN

The silver ran out of Silver Gulch, leaving the town up for grabs. But who was driving families out? Was it Cade, the rancher, or Bishop, the timber boss? Or perhaps Farnsworth, owner of the Five Aces saloon . . . Then ex-New York cop Phil Keyhoe arrived, took a shine to Mary-Jane and decided to stay. First however, he had a mystery to solve and with someone resenting his interference, his life would be in danger every step of the way.

# 1

Riding up with the driver on the swaying stagecoach, Phil Keyhoe's gaze roved across an emptiness of short brown grass reaching to the horizon. He hoped it might look better in the spring. It was a new life he was after, and a fresh start.

The driver said, 'Guess it's your first time travelling west. City man, huh?'

Keyhoe turned his head to study him; husky build, with a weather-beaten face; it was easy to imagine him as one of the early pioneers. He decided the question was asked only out of curiosity.

'Yeah, New York.'

High in the lead-coloured sky, a bird soared, and Keyhoe watched it. Freedom, he thought.

The driver glanced at him. 'Eagle.'

'Empty sort of land.'

'In parts, sure. Other parts are a regular metropolis.' The driver lifted an arm to point to their left; Keyhoe saw only a distant blur. 'That way you've got some homesteads and the Bar C ranch.'

The trail took a right-hand turn, towards the mountains and began a slow climb. The grass thinned, leaving bare stones in places, and the coach rattled.

'Silver Gulch now, where we're stopping for a meal. Couple of years back it was a boom town, plenty of money, plenty of work. All sorts of people rushed here, so many you couldn't count 'em fast enough. People came on foot, on horseback, by wagon, stagecoach, mule, any which way. And one and all thought they were going to get rich on the silver strike.'

'It's over now?'

A dark gloom closed in as the trail rose higher, the slopes covered with tall evergreens, firs and pines set so close together they appeared like a screen.

Keyhoe suddenly missed the bright orange colours of the Fall back east.

The driver spat a stream of brown tobacco juice as if in commentary.

'Some did, most didn't. A few drank and gambled it all away. A few made their pile and cleared off. Then the vein petered out and people began to drift away. There are still some left, of course, but more are leaving all the time.'

The driver cracked his whip above the heads of the horses as the climb steepened. Keyhoe remembered that the inside passenger had called him Wallace when boarding.

'This stage ran daily at one time; now it's weekly. Take the feller riding inside, name of Anson. He's a lawyer and makes regular trips to buy up town lots. Sometimes he's my only passenger going west — he used to travel every week, then it was maybe each second or third week. Now it's monthly.'

Keyhoe looked at the driver. 'Buying lots in town? Is he crazy?'

Wallace grinned. 'Not Anson, no sir — he'll do all right. He's found a mug to buy worthless property, but his percentage is safe, you can bet on that.'

The coach slowed as the trail passed over sun-baked rock, the hooves of the horses clattering and the wheels rattling like tin cans. The coach moved up and down on its braces. Weather-stained pinnacles of rock rose on either side.

Wallace glanced sideways at Keyhoe and said, 'Reckon you got business here, big feller?'

'I'm a travelling man. A dentist.' Keyhoe indicated the carpet bag between his feet on the boot as the seat jolted. 'The tools of my trade.'

Wallace shuddered and measured the size of him, the muscles under hard-wearing dark suiting. 'Waal, I guess no patient of yours is likely to skip paying for your services, and I doubt you'll find much in the way of competition out this way.'

'What I figure — '

Keyhoe stopped as he saw a man on horseback appear from behind the rocks by the side of the trail, just ahead of them. He held a big revolver in one hand and reins in the other; a bandanna was drawn up to hide his face, muffling his voice: 'Pull up, driver. This is a stick-up!'

Keyhoe noted a flannel shirt, wide-brimmed hat, chaps and high-heeled boots with spurs and assumed that the hold-up artist was a cowhand. The horse he rode was small, hardly more than a pony.

Wallace cursed, used the hand brake and hauled back on his reins. It was obviously a case of stop or crash into the horse directly in his path.

'You damned fool,' he yelled. 'We're not carrying any silver — none at all!'

Keyhoe didn't like the way the revolver was wavering from himself to the driver, as if the man holding it couldn't make up his mind which of them to shoot first. He reached down in one easy movement for the shotgun on the floor between Wallace and himself. It had probably seen service when a guard rode up with the driver.

He checked quickly that it was loaded and swung the muzzle around to cover their would-be robber. His finger was on the trigger, ready to squeeze off a shot when Wallace jogged his arm.

'Don't shoot — I know who it is.' The driver leaned over to shout into the coach window. 'Mr Anson, hold your fire — it's only Eddie!'

A muttered comment came from inside. 'It's only Eddie! One day that half-wit will go too far, and that'll be the end of him.'

The hold-up man pulled down his bandanna, grumbling. 'It's not fair. You're not supposed to recognize me. Nobody takes Eddie seriously.' It seemed he might burst into tears any second.

Keyhoe lowered the shotgun slowly, wondering. He saw that Eddie had a caved-in forehead on one side. 'You shouldn't pull stunts like that,' he warned. 'Someone might panic and shoot first.'

'Git outa my way,' Wallace yelled. 'I've still got a schedule to meet — or do you want me to tell Mr Cade about this?' He bit off a lump of chewing tobacco and thrust it into his mouth.

Reluctantly, Eddie steered his horse aside and vanished among the rocks. Wallace released the brake and flicked the reins. The horses leaned into their harness and the stage lurched forward, gathering speed slowly.

'What happened to him?' Keyhoe asked.

'He's a cowboy from the south — they're all Texans at the Bar C. He was on night watch when a storm brewed up and the herd stampeded.'

Wallace chewed vigorously, talking around the tobacco plug as he concentrated on his horses.

'Mostly, when cattle stampede, men get out of their way in a hurry. Eddie was unlucky, his horse put a foot in a gopher hole and threw him right in their path and he got trampled.

'Did you see his forehead? It got caved in by a long-horn's hoof. He's damned lucky to be alive, of course, but he ain't been right in the head since. I mean, who else but Eddie could think of holding up the stage when everybody knows the silver's played out?'

Keyhoe, remembering drunks in the gutters of New York, was tempted to say, 'Quite a few back east.' But that wouldn't have been fair to Eddie. Instead, he asked, 'Who's Mr Cade?'

'Boss of the Bar C ranch. He's not doing so good since Silver Gulch collapsed, but he's not pulling out that I heard of. Them Texans, you've got to admire the way they stick together and look after their own, like Eddie. Mostly he stays outa trouble, but he sure does some mighty strange things at times.'

The coach was pulling easier as the climb began to level off; a few tumbledown buildings showed ahead; some of adobe, others built of logs or planks. Most looked derelict. Phil

Keyhoe had reached the town of Silver Gulch.

'Hold tight,' Wallace warned, and whipped his horses to a gallop.

The stagecoach careered along Main Street, swaying wildly while Wallace yelled 'Yippee . . . ee . . . ee!' He passed a lighted shop front and the marshal's office and town jail — on the point of falling down — and came to a halt with a flourish in front of a sign reading: STAGE POST. The post building had collapsed.

Keyhoe picked up his carpet bag and climbed down on stiff legs. Anson opened the coach door, nodded casually to him and walked away on his own business. Keyhoe had a glimpse of a small man wearing steel-rimmed spectacles, neatly dressed in a dark suit. He wondered how much business a lawyer could get here.

Wallace said, 'Two hour stop-over, if you're going on with me. Restaurant's that way.' He pointed, then unhitched his team and led them down an alley to feed and water them.

Keyhoe stood in inch-thick dust under a steel-grey sky. It's going to be winter real soon, he thought, and shivered.

His gaze roved down one side of the street and up the other side, and he was not impressed. Many of the shacks had never been repaired, with doors sagging and windows taken to use elsewhere. It looked as if people had just walked away after some disaster; false fronts were not quite horizontal and signs had letters missing. The whole place had an abandoned air about it.

It wasn't quite a ghost town, not yet; a few people walked here and there. A general store was open for business under the name Tuttle's. Further on, the Five Aces saloon sounded as though there might still be life in the corpse. But not much.

Beyond the straggling end of town, the trail sloped up towards the mountains that made an impressive background, and dark evergreens closed in to form a gloomy tunnel.

Standing in the dust of Main Street, Keyhoe more or less made up his mind; there was really no point in setting up shop in this quiet and declining town. He'd go on with the coach — but first he'd get a meal. He stepped onto the plankwalk and moved along, opened the door of the restaurant and entered.

It was a long room with two plain wooden tables with benches, one each side of the room; the tables had been scrubbed. At the far end, curtained off, was a glimpse of a kitchen. A chalked notice informed him that beef, apple pie and coffee cost a dollar, and it looked as if the menu hadn't changed lately.

A family, husband, wife and young son ate at one table, their clothes darned and patched. Keyhoe sat on a bench at the other table, back to a wall. An appetizing smell made his mouth water.

A woman came from the kitchen, and he changed his mind about moving on.

# 2

She came directly to his table, a well-set-up woman of, he guessed, about twenty-five. She wore a scrubbed white apron, calf-high boots and a plain thick dress; her hair was tied back but a few stray wisps gave her an elfin charm. Red hair, so she might well have a temper, and that never hurt any woman, Keyhoe thought.

Her complexion had that glow that comes from an outdoor life and her teeth, he noted automatically, were in good condition.

She said, 'Staying over, or travelling through? Just so I know what to order.'

He made a smile. 'Staying, ma'am.'

She smiled back and his heart lifted. 'Only place to eat, so you either like it or get used to it. My customers have to come back.'

'I aim to be a regular.'

She went into the kitchen and he followed her with his eyes. She returned to set a large oval platter before him heaped high with slices of beef in thick gravy; another plate with chunks of home-made bread, and a pitcher of water.

'Bread courtesy of Alice,' she said.

He had no idea who Alice might be, but said gravely, 'Thank Alice for me.'

She gave him another smile as she went to talk to the family at the opposite table and he felt great. The meal was the sort to make dinner in a New York restaurant look like a snack for an invalid. But Phil Keyhoe was a big man so he set to and found she was also a better-than-most cook. The bread was okay too.

He watched her as she chatted to the family at the other table. It was a long time since any woman had made his blood sing like this. He was no stranger to women, but not one had made this sort of impression on him.

She was not, he had to admit, the

sort of beauty to adorn the stage of a theatre, yet there was something magnetic about her; something that appealed strongly to his maleness. He could smell the sweat of her from bending over a wood stove; not a hard woman, but one toughened and tempered by life. He wondered how she managed alone in a mining town — if she was alone.

So he might have competition; he smiled. Competition had never bothered him; he regarded it as a challenge to be taken up.

There was a liveliness in every movement she made, a lilt to her voice — yet, in an unguarded moment he saw sadness cloud her face. Yes, he thought, it would be his job to banish that sadness for ever. She brought him pie and coffee.

It was while he was attacking a giant-sized portion of apple pie that two men strode in. Both had the bowed legs of horsemen.

The man in the lead wore a heavy

jacket and spoke with a commanding voice. 'Mary-Jane, I came as soon as I heard there was a city slicker in town. I stopped at the saloon and talked to Wallace. This new feller been bothering you any?'

He glared around the restaurant, his gaze finally settling on Keyhoe.

'No, he hasn't,' she answered sharply, 'and don't you be bothering my customers, Mr Cade. It's hard enough for a decent woman to make a living here without you scaring folk away.'

'I'll just have a word.' Cade strode across to Keyhoe's table and stared down at him, intent, measuring him. The second cowpuncher followed behind, a revolver holstered at his hip. Both wore high-heeled boots with spurs that jingled.

Keyhoe looked back with interest. This was the Texan rancher who looked after Eddie, a point in his favour. He appeared well into middle-age, some of his muscles running to fat; he cultivated a luxuriant moustache which he preened as he spoke, and there was the smell of whiskey on his breath.

'You,' Cade said. 'You aiming to stay long in Silver Gulch?'

'A while,' Keyhoe answered mildly. 'Thinking of opening a business.'

'Oh?' The rancher looked as if he couldn't believe his ears. 'Opening a business? Here? This town's on the slide, feller.'

'Name's Keyhoe, Mr Cade. My trade's tooth-pulling. If you ever have an aching molar, it pays to be polite to the dentist.'

The man with Cade smiled, took a tobacco sack from his shirt pocket and rolled a brown paper cigarette.

'Name's Logan, Mr Keyhoe,' he drawled. 'I'm foreman of the Bar C, and I'll be sending one of my men to yuh when we're not busy. He's always complaining about a swollen jaw.'

'Any time.' Keyhoe watched Cade's face slowly turning deep red. The boss doesn't like being answered back, he thought.

'I'm warning you, feller, keep your hands to yourself while you're in here. Mary-Jane's off-limits, and I'm here to defend her.'

'I hope I'm always polite to ladies,' Keyhoe said, and finished his coffee.

'See that you are.' Cade nodded brusquely and turned to the cook, who was looking exasperated. 'If you have any trouble, Mary-Jane, let me know right away and I'll run this feller out of town.'

He pushed open the door to the street. Logan winked and followed his boss.

Mary-Jane was talking to his back. 'I don't favour any man, Mr Cade, you or anyone else. And you leave my customers alone!'

Keyhoe smiled at her. 'He means well, I guess.' He paid and reassured her, 'Don't worry about it. I'll be back tomorrow.'

He picked up his carpet bag and went outside. Further along the street, he saw the coach driver coming out of the saloon, and walked that way.

'I'll be staying over,' he said. 'Is there anything resembling a hotel here?'

'See Tuttle's?' Wallace pointed. 'Ask there — and I'll be back in a week if you change your mind.'

'Thanks.' Keyhoe moved along the boardwalk. Even though it was only late afternoon, shadows were lengthening. There was a distinct chill in the air and the almost vertical walls of the gulch seemed to close in, lending the town an air of gloom.

The door of the general store was ajar and he went inside. It was empty of customers, the window dusty; the counter and shelves held a few items left over from a busier time. There were barrels, and sacks on the floor along one wall; pots and pans hung overhead.

Tuttle came from a back room, a small man wearing a large pair of trousers held up by braces, and a shirt without a collar. 'Help yuh?'

'I was told, by Wallace, you're the one to see about a bed.'

The storekeeper was bony, with thinning hair, and skin like a wrinkled apple, but his eyes were still sharp. He measured Keyhoe at a quick glance.

'No bed your size.'

'Never is. I'm used to that.'

Tuttle nodded, as if satisfied this one wouldn't make trouble. He laid a key on the counter.

'Hotel shut months ago, but I've got keys that fit. You can have a room with a bed, no services, a dollar a night in advance. That suit yuh?'

'Guess it'll have to. Is there anyone else staying there now?'

'Lawyer Anson. He won't bother yuh.'

'No, I don't imagine he will.'

Keyhoe paid for a week's lodging, picked up the key and crossed the road to a ramshackle wood building with the sign; OTEL. Some windows were missing and the door stuck; it creaked as he forced it open. The structure was rapidly assuming an air of dereliction and he hoped it wouldn't fall down while he was in it.

Inside he chose an empty room with a single bed and a couple of blankets. He stretched out in his long-johns, legs overhanging the end of the bed, as night clouds gathered and was soon half-dozing. It had been a long day.

But he didn't dream of Mary-Jane. Instead, his past came back to haunt him.

★ ★ ★

Philip Keyhoe was a New York cop, a career cop. He stood six foot four, broad across the chest and hard-muscled. He needed to be to stay alive in the slum areas of the big city, where street gangs ruled and patrolmen walked in pairs.

Keyhoe wanted to be an honest cop, proud of his badge, but that was proving more difficult than he'd supposed. Graft was a way of life. Patrolmen accepted bribes to look the other way when a crime was committed. The sergeant took his cut and advised his men to go easy on the gangs — but the rackets ruined the lives of a lot of people, especially small family shops who had to pay protection or be put out of business.

Keyhoe wanted to do something about it; he tried to uphold the law and help the small man, but it was a losing battle.

The streets and alleys down by the waterfront were narrow and squalid with rubbish. They stank in hot weather, and there was often blood in the gutters. There were drunks and savage dogs.

Keyhoe had been warned: 'You move against the gangs and you're in trouble.' But he persisted in trying to do his sworn duty, to stay honest, and the gangs got fed up with his attitude.

He was patrolling a network of alleys with another cop when half a dozen members of the Hell's Hammers gang came out of the shadows armed with knives and clubs, razors and spikes gripped between their fingers.

The leading hard man said, 'It's Keyhoe we want,' and his partner turned his back and walked away, leaving him to face them alone.

One of the Hammers rushed at Keyhoe with a piece of four-by-two timber, swinging it overhead to use as a club. Keyhoe moved in close and took it away from him. He lowered it horizontally to use as a battering ram and ran it into a man's stomach. He trampled over the body to get out of the alley.

A boy clung like a leech to his back, trying to bring him down by choking him. A razor sliced the air altogether too close.

Keyhoe fought his way free and reached the street where he had room to manoeuvre, set his back to the wall of a building and faced his attackers. There were more of them now. He flung the four-by-two timber at them to give him time to get his truncheon out.

He'd previously opened it to insert a

piece of lead and sewn it up again. It was now a deadly weapon that he swung with deliberate precision.

A nose crunched, streaming blood. A Hammer threw a knife he barely dodged in time; it stuck in the timber wall at his back. Someone dived for his legs and Keyhoe kicked him in the mouth and teeth splattered.

If they brought him down, he'd have no chance. There were too many of the gang for him ever to get up again; and he knew this wasn't just a warning beating. They intended to maim or kill him.

No passer-by stopped to help despite his uniform. It was a silent fight apart from the grunting and swearing of the Hell's Hammers. There was the sound of metal-covered fists hitting meat and Keyhoe felt pain. He sensed his leg throbbing with a new weakness that threatened to give way under him.

His uniform ripped as a blade drew blood, and he kicked out as someone wrapped their arms around his ankles.

The gang came at him, two or three at a time, taking it in shifts, while his arm grew weary wielding the truncheon. He fought back with desperation, struggling to stay on his feet; he inflicted a lot of damage, but other Hammers kept arriving and joining in.

He could feel his leg giving way and knew the end was near.

It was only stupidity that saved him. One of the gang came at him with a tarred stick he had set alight, intending to burn him. But as it was thrust at his face, Keyhoe brushed it aside, and it didn't go out.

The fight dragged on — a bone snapped, a man screamed and then swore — and the improvised torch smouldered and set light to a heap of rubbish piled against the wall. The wood planks caught and spectators at the back set up a shout: 'Fire!'

Some of the Hammers fled and Keyhoe managed to stay upright until a fire engine arrived with a great clanging of a brass bell. Firemen unreeled a hose and turned a jet of water on both the fire and the fighters. Only then did he allow himself to slide down the wall to the ground.

When he came out of hospital, he still had a limp. His sergeant told him, 'Let's hope that taught you a lesson. Maybe now you'll take money when it's offered. See that you keep your nose clean in future — we don't need troublemakers.'

Keyhoe listened to him and decided that his days of trying to be an honest cop on the streets of New York were over. He handed in his badge and thought of wide open spaces out west where a man could breathe fresh air.

That was when he saw a newspaper ad for an apprenticeship in dentistry. He counted up his money and applied . . .

# 3

Keyhoe awoke with a faint grey light seeping through a grimy window pane and wondered, for a moment, where he was. His dream faded to be replaced by the memory of Mary-Jane and he rose and dressed quickly.

After visiting the outhouse and sluicing cold water over his face at the pump, Keyhoe heard Anson moving about in his room and knocked on the door.

'Sorry to bother you, Mr Anson, but as you're a regular here, I'm hoping you can advise me about some basic things like — '

'Certainly I will. Come in. Not buying up town lots, I hope?'

'No sir, that's not my line of business at all. I'm just a travelling tooth-puller, but I reckon to smarten up some.'

Anson smiled. 'Yes, Mary-Jane does

have that effect, doesn't she? I keep a small stove here to heat water, so bring your razor and help yourself — there's even a bit of mirror. You're absolutely right, we professional men must keep up appearances.'

He polished his spectacles on a clean white handkerchief. 'If you need anything, the man to see is Tuttle. Amongst other things, he's also the mayor.'

Keyhoe paused at the door. 'I must admit I'm curious — why's your client so interested in what amounts to a ghost town?'

The lawyer shrugged. 'I never concern myself over the peculiarities of clients. If they want me to buy town lots, I do just that. If they ask my advice, of course, that's a different matter.'

He handed the key of his room to Keyhoe. 'Now I'm away to breakfast and to see if any more good citizens are selling. Lock up when you're done, and hand the key to Tuttle.'

He walked away, humming cheerfully.

Keyhoe shaved carefully, dusted down his clothes and set off to the restaurant for breakfast. In Main Street he saw a family loading their few possessions onto a cart hitched to a mule. The man looked unhappy, the woman fed up; only the young boy seemed to regard their leaving as an adventure.

As he passed by, Keyhoe heard the man say, 'There isn't any ghost. That's nonsense, only a bar-room story — '

'Saw it,' said the boy.

'Shut up, son. I won't have you scaring your mother again.'

Keyhoe was about to move on when a revolver shot sounded and a voice yelled, 'Stop right there!'

Startled, he looked round to see a strange figure hurrying along the centre of the street in short strides that kicked up the dust. The figure approached, waving a revolver in the air.

His first thought was that this must

be one of the old prospectors he'd heard about who lived too much alone. Then he realized the figure was not that of a man at all, and was addressing, not him, but the family. Intrigued, he lingered.

The strange figure was that of a middle-aged woman whose face might have once been used as a battering ram. She dressed like a man in patched denim trousers and faded wool shirt with a shapeless hat pushed to the back of her head.

The family man grabbed the reins of the mule to stop it bolting. 'Quit shouting, Alice,' he said. 'You'll panic the animal.'

'Panic, who's panicking I'd like to know? Not me. No one's getting me out of my place without a fight. Not Anson, not anybody.' She spoke quickly in a high-pitched voice.

'You can't change my mind, Alice. There's no future here. We're moving on because there's no silver, and that's the only reason. Now stand aside while we finish loading.'

Alice glowered belligerently. 'If I ever meet this so-called ghost he'll become one pronto!'

She turned a buffalo's glare on Keyhoe. 'Where'd you spring from? I suppose you're another of these idiots who believe this ghost nonsense?'

'No, ma'am. Can't say as I do, but I've met people who'd believe anything.'

Yes, he thought, the streets of New York were full of con men who took advantage of the mugs. But he hadn't expected to encounter a ghost in Silver Gulch.

Anson was just leaving the restaurant and started along the plankwalk. He saw Keyhoe and Alice and the family and hesitated; then he came on.

As he reached them, Alice snarled, 'Proud of yourself, are you, Mr Anson? Driving another poor family out of town.'

He tipped his hat. 'Not guilty,' he said pleasantly. 'When someone decides to sell, I buy. Are you ready to sell yet, Alice?'

'Never! Try your tricks on me, and I'll fill yuh full of lead.'

He sighed. 'No tricks, Alice, I promise. I'm a lawyer, that's all. I take instructions from my client.'

'Lawyer!' She spat in the dust. 'No need for any lawyer where there's no law.'

Anson nodded to Keyhoe in a friendly way and walked on. Keyhoe continued to the restaurant, went in and sat down. Mary-Jane brought flapjacks.

He thought she looked down this morning and kept quiet, so there were just the two of them when she brought his coffee.

'I noticed there's another family packing up and leaving this morning,' he said.

She nodded, but her smile appeared forced. 'Yes, I heard. They're nervous. Some of the women get so scared they demand their men take them some-where else, anywhere else.'

'I overheard talk of a ghost — '

'I don't like that word . . . if you don't mind, talk about something else.'

Keyhoe raised an eyebrow. 'Why, sure, ma'am,' he said easily, and racked his memory for whatever he could remember of the fashions women wore back east.

When he left, he asked casually, 'Who's Alice?'

Now Mary-Jane smiled. 'You've met Alice already, have you? I'll ask you to remember she's a friend, no matter how she looks. She's let herself go a bit since her husband — another miner — walked away and left her stranded here, so she's not that keen on men.'

'Understandable.'

'But she's a good person. Nowadays she has a bakery — and runs a poker school in the backroom.'

She hesitated, her eyes searching his.

'Sometimes Alice invites a cowhand to stay overnight, but that's none of our business.'

'Agreed. Any friend of yours is a friend of mine,' Keyhoe said, and added, 'If anything scares you, Mary-Jane, call on me. Phil Keyhoe's my name.'

He left the restaurant and moved casually along the boardwalk towards the store, thinking: there's more going on in this town than appears on the surface.

Tuttle was standing in his doorway when Keyhoe arrived, frowning after the mule-drawn cart pulling out of Silver Gulch.

'Morning,' Keyhoe said. 'Looks like this could be a regular ghost town soon.'

The storekeeper nodded.

'The family leaving said something about seeing a ghost.'

'Some claim to.' Sharp eyes watched him. 'D'you happen to believe in ghosts?'

'Not me,' Keyhoe said, 'but Mary-Jane seemed a mite upset.'

'Not surprising. The story goes — you

understand, I don't believe a word of this.'

Keyhoe nodded.

'The story goes that some see the ghost of a miner. This was when the mine was working, of course. There was a flood and a rockfall and men were trapped below ground. They're still down there . . . '

Tuttle went on after a pause. 'And Mary-Jane's husband was one of them. It's the reason she won't leave.'

'A bar-room story?'

'Likely enough, but you won't convince those who want to believe.'

Tuttle hitched up his trousers. 'Step inside for a coffee. Unless you've got business elsewhere?'

'I'll take the coffee. Heard you were mayor.'

Tuttle almost laughed. 'Yeah, I guess I still am. It meant something when I got elected, but not now. It's just that I've never been unelected.'

The store was no more busy than it had been the day before. Tuttle already had a coffee pot on the stove and he filled two pint-sized mugs. Keyhoe sipped cautiously and found it black, sweet and strong.

'Surprised nobody got off their tail and chased this feller playing ghost,' he said.

'Town used to have a marshal till the silver ran out. He was one of the first to leave. There are very few left now, mostly folk who came intending to settle. Those quick to come after the silver were quick to go.'

The storekeeper looked sad, then brightened. 'We were lucky the trouble-makers left early on — likely following the marshal to another boom town.'

He pointed at the cracker barrel.

'Help yourself . . . yeah, the town's starting to fall apart. There are still a few prospectors higher up the gulch, but little hope of another strike.'

'Yet people like yourself are still here. How come?'

Tuttle looked hard at him for a moment, then changed the subject.

'Heard you were setting up as a dentist.'

'That's right. What I need first is an office and — '

'Plenty of empty shacks around. Help yourself. I've got a yard broom you can borrow.'

' — and a big chair, with arm rests a patient can grip hold of.'

Tuttle went into the back room and returned, pushing a solid-looking chair in front of him. He seemed to be moving slowly and carefully.

'Stiff joints,' he said. 'I'd say there was rain coming before long.'

Keyhoe looked the chair over and said, 'This'll do fine. How much?'

'You can borrow it for now. If you open an office, the town might look as if it meant to survive. Let's see how long you last.'

Keyhoe went up and down the street and selected a wood shack across from the store and saloon. It had a high false front that impressed him and the roof didn't have a hole in it.

He swept it out and moved his chair in. There was already a small table where he could lay out his tools; all it needed was a good scrub.

'How'd yuh spell your name?' Tuttle yelled from across the street. 'I'll paint a sign for you to nail up.'

As Keyhoe told him, hoofbeats and rebel yells sounded from the south end of Main Street, echoing between the buildings. He looked out and saw a small figure running desperately through the dust, pursued by cowboys on ponies shouting and firing revolvers in the air.

Keyhoe frowned. The running man was Chinese and he was almost out of breath. When the quarry reached the doorway where he stood, he said, 'In here, son.'

The Chinese man darted past him, into the shack, and crouched low behind the chair. Keyhoe stood in the doorway, filling it. The cowboys rode up, swung from their saddles and came swaggering towards him.

'Outa the way, feller. We want the Chinee.'

Keyhoe did not move. 'That so? What do you want him for?' he asked pleasantly.

'Goin' to cut off his pigtail,' the cowboy in the lead said, pulling a knife from his belt.

'Now why on earth would you want to do that? It seems an odd sort of thing to do.'

'He's a Chinee, ain't he?'

'So?'

'We always cut off their pigtails when we catch them. Now stand aside.'

'Not sure I can do that. Seems a lot of you to deal with one small boy.'

'He's no boy — he's a miner.'

The Texans seemed puzzled. No one had interfered with their fun before. Cutting off pigtails was what they always did when they caught one on his own.

'It don't hurt,' a cowboy explained carefully. 'It's just a bit of fun. The regular thing.'

'Perhaps it's not fun for him.' Keyhoe looked them over. Neither Cade nor Logan was with them, but he saw Eddie at the back, hitching horses to a rail.

'Aren't you ashamed of yourself, Eddie?' he called. 'Does it take a whole pack of you to run down one little feller?'

Eddie turned around to look at him, then ducked low to hide behind other cowboys. He said nothing.

The Texans began to crowd him, trying to get into the shack. Keyhoe stood like a rock.

'Big feller,' the nearest cowpuncher drawled, 'You're in the way. I'm not arguing, I'm telling yuh.' He unholstered his revolver and pointed it. 'Stand aside, or I'll let daylight through yuh!'

# 4

'We're going to have that pigtail!'

Keyhoe, facing the crowd of angry cowpunchers, smiled. The Texan holding a revolver on him was carelessly close; it needed only one step forward and he took the gun by its barrel from the surprised man's hand, and said, 'No.'

For a few seconds, there was only astonishment, then it looked as if they might rush him. He reversed the gun and waited, finger around the trigger.

It was a tense moment. Then a welcome diversion came as a wagon carrying a full load of timber creaked its way down the dusty street. The man beside the driver frowned at the cowboys. 'Pull up,' he ordered, and the wagon stopped.

'What's going on here?'

'Try minding your own business,

Bishop,' a cowboy drawled.

The man called Bishop stepped down into the road. Three rough-looking men in flannel and denim jumped off the wagon to join him.

'Anything that happens in this town is my business,' Bishop said, and Keyhoe relaxed slightly. He felt he was no longer entirely alone.

'I asked a question,' Bishop said in a powerful voice, 'and I expect an answer. What's going on here?' He jabbed a finger at one cowboy. 'You, speak up.'

Bishop had broad shoulders that filled out a corduroy suit and large red hands. He took a cigar from an inside pocket, bit off one end and lit it. All the time he stared directly at the one cowboy he had picked on.

'Just hazing a Chinee, is all. This feller here's trying to stop us having fun.'

Bishop switched his attention to Keyhoe. He was a man used to assessing the worth of others and didn't appear impressed.

'I'm all for a bit of fun myself, like a

good fight when it's one against one with bare knuckles. Suppose you pick one of your Texans and set to? I'll see the rest don't take a hand, big feller — and we'll make up a purse for the winner.'

There was some muttering among the cowboys, but they finally agreed on a champion: a tall lean *hombre* with a flat stomach and thin leather gloves on his hands. He had muscles but was probably more at home on a horse.

'Okay, Dave, take him apart!'

Keyhoe returned the revolver, slipped off his jacket and hung it over the back of the chair. He spoke quietly to the small Chinese, 'See if you can disappear while they're watching the show.'

Dave handed his Stetson to a pal and advanced to meet him. Keyhoe waited patiently, watching. He was a deliberate fighter, favouring a study of his opponent, and then responding.

It was quickly obvious why Dave had been chosen. He was light on his feet and moved easily, darting in to attack and then dancing back out of range. They were matched in height, but Keyhoe had the advantage of weight.

He advanced into the casual ring formed by the crowd. He pushed out his right fist and Dave swayed around it. He kept advancing, punching, till Dave couldn't back any further. Then he hit him a sledgehammer blow.

Dave staggered, recovered and began seriously to fight back. Still Keyhoe waited, studying his opponent.

Bishop, impatient, called, 'Come on, big feller, murder him — I want to see blood.'

Keyhoe ignored the commentary and fought his own way. He soon found an advantage; Dave wore high-heeled boots that made it awkward for him to retain his balance.

'Stop prancing around, Dave, and hit him,' one of the cowhands shouted.

Keyhoe kept after him, pressing his advantage, using his weight behind every punch and keeping him off balance.

'Two to one the big feller,' Bishop said, and some Texans took the bet.

Keyhoe decided to finish the fight and went in with hammering fists; left-right to the body, an uppercut to the jaw. Dave's eyes glazed and his knees sagged; he swayed, almost out on his feet.

'Finish him,' Bishop shouted excitedly. 'Kill him — kill him!'

Only Keyhoe's fist was holding Dave up. He stepped back and the cowboy dropped in a heap in the dust.

'Hell,' murmured a Texan. 'Never seen anyone drop Dave like that before.'

'Really?' remarked one of Bishop's men, with a big knife sheathed at his waist. 'I could drop him in half that time any day.'

'Not in a straight fight, Gregson.'

'Kick his head in,' Bishop bawled at Keyhoe. 'Use your boots!'

'No need for that,' he said mildly. 'I won your bet for you.'

'Yeah, well . . . ' Bishop made an obvious effort to hide his blood lust and swept off his hat. 'Come on, you sporting men, chuck some money in the hat for the winner.' He went around the crowd collecting coins and a few notes and both loggers and cowboys contributed something.

As he handed the money to Keyhoe, a high-pitched voice cut in: 'You big bully — shame on you for picking on my Dave!' Alice arrived, looking fierce. 'If you've hurt him, you'll answer to me!'

She helped Dave to his feet. He was wobbly and leaned on her for support; he spat out a tooth, blood dribbling from his mouth.

Someone laughed. 'You oughta see a dentist about that, Dave!'

Tuttle came pushing his way through the crowd with a crudely painted sign, hammer and nails. 'You've got one, boys. Let me inform you, we have another professional man in Silver Gulch, opening up his shop.'

He hurriedly nailed up the sign he had painted:

Bishop paused in collecting his bets, and looked carefully at Keyhoe. 'You could have fooled me. Step into the saloon and I'll buy you a drink.'

A cowboy peered inside the shack. 'That little yellow man's gone while we watched the fight.' He looked and sounded disgusted.

Keyhoe smiled. 'I'll be pleased to accept that beer, Mr Bishop.'

'You sound like a Yankee, so welcome. Anyone who takes these damned Texans down a peg is okay with me.'

'Thought the war was over,' Keyhoe said easily.

He split the prize money into roughly two halves and looked for Dave. The cowpuncher was being helped away by Alice and he hurried after them. He shoved half the money at her, and said, 'This is for Dave. We'll split it — we were pushed into that fight by Bishop.'

As he turned away, she looked at him

with loathing, but still grabbed the money.

'Don't think that buys you anything,' she shouted after him as he hastened after Bishop into the Five Aces saloon.

'All drinks are on me,' Bishop boomed. 'This boy won a bet for me, beating hell out of a goddamned Southerner.'

'That so?' the saloonkeeper said in a neutral tone, though Keyhoe thought he detected a hint of Southern drawl. 'Waal, now, in here we keep the peace.'

He brought a club that was almost a small tree-trunk from below the counter. 'Anyone for fighting moves outside. What'll you have, stranger?'

'Name's Keyhoe, and I'll take a small beer.'

The cattlemen and the Northerners sat at separate tables on opposite sides of the saloon. Keyhoe observed that the boastful tough guy called Gregson sat close to Bishop. He remembered the wagon they'd arrived on.

'Are you in timber, Mr Bishop?'

'Mr Timber in person,' he replied. 'I own the sawmill and I've got the loggers on my payroll. Anyone wants timber around here, they come to me; building, firing, whatever. I still ship out enough to keep going, unlike those who scare easy.'

'I take it you don't believe in this alleged ghost?'

'You take it wrong. I was one of the first to see it. So what? Dead men can't hurt me or my business.'

Keyhoe heard the batwing doors squeal as someone pushed them open. He saw the saloon-keeper glance in the big mirror behind the bar. A man in a dirt-stained coverall came into the saloon, looked around and headed for Keyhoe's table.

'Are you the tooth man? I've got one giving me a lot of pain. How much do you charge?'

'Two dollars.'

The man fumbled in a pocket and brought out some coins. 'Let's get it over with.'

'I advise taking a stiff dose of whiskey first.'

The saloon-keeper poured whiskey into a tumbler. 'On the house, Mr Nickson.'

Keyhoe and his first patient crossed the street, Nickson clutching the tumbler. A number of the curious followed them.

'If you'll sit in the chair, please. And do try to relax.'

The audience crowded the doorway and consisted mostly of cowboys. 'You should eat more beef, Nickson. It's all those vegetables you grow that rot your teeth!'

Keyhoe waited till his patient swallowed more whiskey, then asked, 'How d'you feel now?'

'It's deadened the pain.'

'Right then, grip the chair arms — both hands — and hold tight. Open your mouth. Wider . . . wider!'

Keyhoe selected his forceps and tapped gently on a tooth.

'Ow . . . yes, that one!'

Keyhoe got a knee on the patient's stomach to hold him in place and pushed the forceps into his mouth, bearing down. He remembered the words of his master: 'Push the forceps hard, to get down to the root. Ease the tooth out with a rocking motion . . . insert the tool between the gum and the tooth . . . take a firm grip.'

He'd done this before, in the dental office, under instruction. But now he was on his own, in front of an audience. Then, he'd had the use of an anaesthetic, and whiskey was not recommended — but there was nothing else available here.

Nickson struggled, Keyhoe persevered and the cowboys cheered him on. To them it was first class entertainment.

'Hold that nester down, big feller — don't let him make a bolt for it!'

'Mighty glad it's not me in that chair!'

'Reckon Dave got his tooth out the easy way!'

'Why don't yuh take 'em all out while you're at it? Save a heap of time!'

Keyhoe was lucky and the tooth came out in one go.

'Okay, use the spittoon. And you can take some more whiskey if you want.'

'Jesus . . . ' Nickson looked pale and shaken, and held his jaw in his hand.

Keyhoe said, 'Keep taking the whiskey. Rest, if you can. Wash your mouth out after you eat and try to keep your teeth clean — here, have a toothpick. The pain will wear off after a while, and then you'll be glad you had it out.'

Nickson staggered away, looking unhappy, and Keyhoe crossed Main Street to the saloon. His audience had gone, and so had their horses.

He felt like celebrating his first success, but the loggers, too, had gone.

'Small beer,' he ordered.

The saloon-keeper put a glass under a barrel and turned a tap. He said, 'Bishop went to eat. He fancies himself as Mary-Jane's protector — as I do myself, of course. The name's Farnsworth, by the way.'

'Nice to meet you, Mr Farnsworth.'

The saloon-keeper laughed, showing teeth like a shark. He wore a long black coat, brushed clean, white shirt and string tie. His face was pale and thin and he cultivated sideboards. His eyes held a glint.

'Few say that, Mr Keyhoe.'

His long thin fingers produced a pack of cards from beneath the counter; he shuffled, cut and dealt two hands with the smooth precision of a professional gambler.

'You a poker player?'

'Not with a card sharp.'

'Ah, you can read signs. Well, well, an educated dentist. But you needn't worry, I only need to cheat when playing against cheats. I win against amateurs simply because I'm a pro.'

Without warning, and too fast for Keyhoe to see how it was done, a small Derringer pistol appeared in Farnsworth's hand as if by magic.

'I have a thing about cheats,' he said.

'How is it you're running a saloon?'

'I own the place.' His teeth showed again in his shark-like grin. 'Won it on a bet.'

Keyhoe sipped his beer slowly, standing at the bar counter. 'I still wonder why people stay here. It seems to me, so far, that only Bishop has anything like a going business.'

'True. Let's say we're a bit slow to believe the worst ... except for Mary-Jane. Now I'd say she doesn't believe ... but just suppose it was real and the ghost of her old man? She may have a bit of doubt there. He was likeable, was Riley, with a gift of the blarney. My guess is she doesn't find it so easy to shrug him off. The grieving widow.'

It was said in a light-hearted way and Keyhoe couldn't be sure how serious he was, but it gave him something to think about.

Something besides the men who stayed on in Silver Gulch. Did they know something those leaving didn't?

He finished his beer and walked towards the restaurant. He found Bishop talking earnestly to Mary-Jane. Gregson was with him, and Keyhoe didn't like the way the logger looked at her. He sat on the bench at the other table, watching Gregson and listening to Bishop.

'Saw it myself, didn't I?' the timber boss said. 'Not close enough to recognize a face, but dressed the way a miner does — heavy boots, helmet, thick trousers and shirt. If it's someone dressing up to play at ghost, it has to be crazy Eddie. Who else could it be? No one else would pull a trick like that.'

'Who else?' Mary-Jane said, and turned away. 'That's a good question.'

Bishop left, closely followed by Gregson, and Mary-Jane served Keyhoe's meal with a smile.

'Thanks for helping Wu. I don't like it when somebody they see as a bit different — Wu, Eddie, anyone — gets picked on.'

Keyhoe said, 'Reckon I might try to find out who it is playing ghost.'

'I can only approve that idea,' she said. 'It's too bad that some *hombre* has been scaring womenfolk away. I'd like to see him nailed.'

'You're sure?'

'I guess you heard.' She smiled faintly. 'My husband was killed down the mine. I don't believe in ghosts — at least, I don't think I do — but there is that small element of doubt.'

She looked up at him with a hopeful expression. 'If you're serious, the place to start is the north end of town. That's where those people who say they saw something were at the time.'

'I'm dead serious. I aim to remove that element of doubt, Mary-Jane.'

Keyhoe left the restaurant, walked to his hotel room and stretched out on the bed for a nap before starting on his ghost hunt.

# 5

It was growing dark when Keyhoe left the hotel and moved quietly along the alley behind Main Street. There was no boardwalk here, only dirt. North end of town she had said; that was where the ghost was supposed to appear.

When he thought of Mary-Jane, he realized he had misread the situation. It was not Cade, or Bishop, or Farnsworth who were his rivals for her love; it was a dead man. She was still in love with her husband, and that gave a whole new point to laying this ghost. The sooner the better, he decided.

He picked his way among discarded junk, careful to avoid making unnecessary noise. Sound could travel a long way and, if the ghost was going to walk, he didn't want to warn off whoever it was.

Near the town limits he slowed his

pace even further, putting one foot cautiously in front of another. There wasn't much light left and the towering walls of the gorge seemed to press closer about him. It confined his view of the world to a narrow strip. Shadows were darker and the few stars bright spots in a black sky.

Some of the empty shacks were crudely built, just four log walls and a roof cut from sod. Others were at the point of collapse, windows gone, doors hanging.

A musty smell hung over the area, and a tiny animal scuttled out of his path. He paused, listening. Was that only a rusty hinge in the breeze?

Cloud covered the stars, and the darker patches might be anything. The cloud moved on — why was that shadow moving?

He had almost decided to give up. Disused mine workings were dangerous and he began to appreciate that he should have explored the area in daylight first. Then he thought he heard a footfall, soft as a feather landing. He waited, and it was too easy to imagine things.

Holding his breath, straining his ears to their limit, he stared into the gloom. Something white glimmered, swaying to and fro in the twilight. It was very faint. If it was the person scaring women out of town, Keyhoe wanted to get his hands on him.

It was vaguely spherical, like a face hanging in mid-air, unsupported. He heard a low moaning sound, like an animal in pain and, despite his lack of belief, the wailing raised his scalp. No wonder some people had been scared out of their wits, and out of town.

He drew his lead-weighted truncheon and stepped silently towards the apparition. Now he could make out a human figure, dusty white, in rough clothing. Definitely spooky, he thought grimly.

His foot struck a discarded can and, at the sudden noise, the ghostly shape turned away.

Keyhoe cursed and ran forward. Now the faint figure turned dark, vanishing before his eyes. His hope of dragging this person before Mary-Jane disappeared. 'Damn, damn, damn!'

He threw his truncheon. Perhaps it hit, more likely it didn't. He couldn't be sure. The evening gloom was nearly night-black and the ghost had gone. He searched, but found no body.

He groped around for his truncheon in the dark and located its smooth shape among the rubble. He moved from one deserted shack to another, peered behind mounds of rubbish. He saw no one and, disgusted, made his way back to the town. On the way to his hotel he passed the baker's shop, an oil lamp glowing in the window. Alice stared out at him, frowning.

*  *  *

Cade rode the range studying the grass, too short and too burnt by the sun. He looked at the sky and wished for rain.

Locating here had seemed like a good idea at the time, and it still was, he reminded himself, compared to the alternative.

He could remember Texas and the dust on the long trail north to the cowtowns, the trains that carried steers east to market. Year after year he got a good price, though it was obvious this couldn't last. More settlers were moving west, putting up fences and using the water for crops.

The trails got longer as the cowtowns moved further west, and the price for longhorn beef fell as more ranchers began to breed fat Hereford cattle. And he wasn't getting any younger.

So he'd taken the decision to sell up, moved his herd north with the few cowhands who wanted to come with him, and started again. Then Silver Gulch had been a booming market, until the vein ran out.

Staying was now a matter of being reluctant to take another decision; that and Mary-Jane.

He tried to give the impression he regarded her as the daughter he'd never had; in public, he made a big deal of offering her his protection. But he knew that wasn't the truth. He felt younger when he looked at her; she stirred his blood and made him feel it was time to settle down and raise a family.

Of course, there was Bishop, and Farnsworth . . .

His horse pricked its ears and looked towards the river. Cade straightened in the saddle as he saw a rider coming towards him and recognized Logan. His foreman arrived at an easy lope and reined in.

'Most of the herd's along the river bank. Water level's down again. Sure hope we get rain soon.'

They sat at ease and studied the sky without much hope while Logan rolled a cigarette.

Logan was younger than his boss, with the better eyesight, and spoke almost casually: 'Riders.'

Cade looked to the south. The two

horsemen were strangers, with packs behind their saddles. Both wore long coats with dark flat hats. Despite the dust of travel each was clean-shaven and not openly carrying hand weapons. One, the older of the two, had a rifle — for hunting game? — behind his saddle. There was a similarity about their faces as if they might be brothers.

Their horses looked as if they'd come a long way at an easy pace. As they came closer, Cade noted their hands, smooth and pale-skinned. They were not the hands of men used to outdoor work, or looking for it.

They paused, and he said, 'You're crossing Bar C land.' He preened his moustache.

The older of the two strangers said pleasantly, 'Crossing is about right. Travelling through.'

Cade nodded. 'That's okay then.' He failed to place the man's accent, Southern, but not Texan.

The younger of the two drawled, 'Looking for a poker game, sir. Heard tell there's a real professional in these parts.'

Now he had it. A touch of French. He noted that Logan had put out his cigarette and that his hand was close to the butt of his Colt.

He said, 'Unusual. Never heard of anyone travelling to find a pro to play against. Professionals usually win.'

'Perhaps not this time. Perhaps we just want to gain experience.'

Cade felt vaguely uneasy, and looked from one to the other. It was nothing he could put his finger on; both seemed relaxed and easy-going.

'The only class player around here is a gambler named Farnsworth, and he runs the saloon in Silver Gulch.'

'Ah, much silver?'

'Not now, it's played out.'

'Well, no mind.' The speaker sounded pleased. 'Poker's our game, and I sure do thank you, sir. Now, if you'll point us towards this Silver Gulch, we'll be travelling on.'

Cade pointed. 'You need to take the

trail going up into the mountains.'

As the strangers rode away the older one touched the brim of his hat. The younger man murmured a few words in French.

Cade had picked up a smattering of the language, enough to grasp the meaning: 'At last!'

Logan stared after them. 'Can't say I much like the look of that pair. You don't often see a Sharps rifle these days.'

'No, you don't,' Cade said, and thought about it.

The Sharps had been designed to fire .50 calibre bullets; it was the gun buffalo hunters used, and could stop a two-thousand-pound bison charging at thirty miles an hour. He considered what such a bullet would do to a man, and said, 'Farnsworth can take care of himself.'

*   *   *

Keyhoe ambled up Main Street as the sun was getting high. He had deliberately left getting a meal until late in the hope of finding Mary-Jane on her own. A solitary horse was hitched outside the Five Aces, and there were two customers inside Tuttle's. Must be Saturday, he thought, and smiled. He'd lost track of the day of the week and it didn't matter here.

He dawdled, anticipating the pleasure of Mary-Jane's company. He crossed the road and climbed onto the boardwalk. As he approached the door of the restaurant, he heard sounds of a struggle; the screech of wood as a table shifted, sobbing breaths and a gasped curse. He quickened his pace, flung open the door and stepped inside.

Mary-Jane was fighting a burly figure in a red flannel shirt and denim pants, and her attacker was not getting it all his own way. Her boots scraped down his shin and her fingernails raked his face.

'Bitch!' the man snarled, and balled his hand to hit her.

Keyhoe grasped him by the shoulder and hauled him back, spinning him off-balance. Mary-Jane broke free.

Keyhoe smelt whiskey on the man's breath and recognized him as Gregson, the logger who had sat next to Bishop. 'Outside,' he said.

'Bastard, giving me orders!'

Gregson pulled a Bowie knife from its sheath at his belt and lunged at Keyhoe, who stepped back as the broad blade swept towards him. It was a big heavy knife that could make a serious wound if it struck flesh and blood.

Mary-Jane said, 'Don't be a fool, Gregson. You know what will happen to you if I report this to Mr Bishop.'

The logger laughed, ignoring her warning. He lashed out again with the knife at Keyhoe. 'Scared, huh? After I cut your liver out, I'll deal with that spitfire. Can't allow her to think she's too good for — '

Keyhoe pulled out his truncheon and rapped sharply on the wrist of the bully's knife-hand; the blade clattered to the floor and Keyhoe kicked it away. He lowered his truncheon to use as a ram and shoved it hard into Gregson's stomach, bringing him to a standstill, doubled over and gasping for air.

Keyhoe gripped him by the arms, swung him around, and shoved. Gregson flew through the doorway, narrowly missing Farnsworth who stepped aside, Derringer in hand. He landed heavily in thick dust beyond the plankwalk.

'You again,' Farnsworth said. 'You've been warned before. You'll get no more liquor at my saloon. Now get the hell out of town and stay out.'

'Are you all right, Mary-Jane?' Keyhoe asked. He picked up Gregson's knife by the hilt and snapped the blade under his boot.

She had straightened her clothes and now ran a comb through her hair. 'He was drunk,' she said calmly. 'Thanks for your help.'

Farnsworth put his small gun back in its shoulder holster. 'I don't know why Bishop hired that one — he's nothing but trouble.'

Gregson picked himself up out of the

dirt. He'd got his breath back but, unarmed, he wasn't about to go up against Farnsworth and that other one, the big feller who claimed to be a dentist.

He scowled at Keyhoe. 'I'll be back, bastard, and I'll get you.' He shambled off, swaying.

Keyhoe put away his truncheon. 'Not if I see you first.'

'Make sure you do,' Farnsworth drawled. 'He's not the sort to come at you from the front, so watch your back.'

He smiled at Mary-Jane and, as he walked away, added, 'Seems like you've got yourself another champion.'

Alice came hurrying from across the road, drawing her revolver. 'Are you okay, Mary-Jane?' she shouted.

She fired a bullet into the ground at Gregson's heels. 'You can move faster than that — git!'

Swearing viciously, the logger broke into a shambling run, heading north out of town.

Alice stared suspiciously at Keyhoe.

'This ape bothering yuh?'

'Mr Keyhoe saved me from Gregson. Mr Farnsworth came to help.'

'Huh,' Alice sniffed. 'Don't trust any of 'em. Men, they're all the same — only want one thing. Forget Gregson, he's a nothing. It's his boss you need to watch. Have you seen that fortress of his? No? It's huge, and he's after you to run it for him!'

'I'll be all right,' Mary-Jane insisted, and added, to Keyhoe, 'Come inside and sit down. I'll get your meal now.'

Keyhoe straightened the table and bench and sat down. She bustled away, returning with a large steak and a plate of fresh vegetables. 'From Nickson,' she said. 'He grows all sorts on his homestead.'

'Nice,' he said.

He ate hungrily and, over coffee, said, 'I saw your so-called ghost, and I'm sure it's somebody dressed up — but I've got to admit it was pretty scary. Unfortunately, whoever it was got away from me. But I promise you he won't next time.'

'You're sure it was a person disguised? Why would anyone do that?'

'I'm sure. I wonder why anyone would want to buy town lots, and who it is.'

*   *   *

While it was still daylight, Keyhoe rambled around North End, making a mental map of the area. He didn't intend the ghost to elude him next time.

He soon realized how lucky he'd been not to have had a serious accident; there was more than one old shaft loosely boarded over.

Where the town finally ended, the trail started up again, more steeply, towards the mountains; and here he saw the stumps of trees that had been cut. He stared upwards, working on a shred of meat with a toothpick, thinking; Bishop's sawmill must be up there somewhere.

Bishop, and Gregson. Gregson brought Mary-Jane to mind and nudged him back to business. The mine workings were gradually rusting away, the sod roofs over neglected shanties collapsed. Everywhere there was discarded metal and timber, broken picks and shovels. Abandoned huts had warped in the weather and vacant windows made dark holes like eyes that watched him. The area, now falling apart, was more extensive than he'd realized.

He found the spot where the ghost had disappeared and inspected it closely. He found traces of a white powder on the ground, and he stooped and wet his finger and cautiously tasted it.

Flour? Was it as simple as that, how the ghost made himself visible in the dark?

A baker used flour . . . so why had he assumed the person playing ghost must be a man?

Passing one shack, he fancied he glimpsed a small pale face staring at him from a broken window; then it vanished. Wu? What was the Chinese guy doing hiding here?

# 6

Mary-Jane was clearing up after another of Keyhoe's late breakfasts, and she was alone in the restaurant. Being alone after her husband's death had not bothered her before; most people had been kind, and supportive, especially Alice.

There was always something to do; wood for the stove, provisions, preparing food to cook, washing up, cleaning. But now, with this ghost business . . . of course, she didn't believe, but it was hard to turn her back and walk away. Just suppose . . .

No, she didn't believe it. They'd had a good marriage; surely Riley wouldn't come back to haunt her?

Alice wasn't around as much as she used to be either. Not since Keyhoe had arrived.

She smiled at the thought, but it was true what they said: life had to go on and, when she thought of him, her heart lifted. She hoped he would soon catch whoever it was playing ghost; then perhaps she could shed the past like an old skin and make a fresh start.

It wasn't Wu, she felt sure. He lived where he could, with a handful of her left-overs and, she suspected, stale bread from Alice. He also took in a bit of laundry. Keyhoe had waited again last night but seen nothing. He would try another time.

She wondered, why did the ghost appear some nights and not others? That was another mystery.

The door opened and two men walked in, strangers in long coats with dusty flat hats. The older one carried a big rifle. Hunters? They were clean-shaven and the older one smiled and removed his hat.

'Can we get a meal here, ma'am?' he asked politely.

She smiled back. 'That's what I'm here for. It's beef and potatoes, pie and coffee.'

'That'll be fine, ma'am.'

They sat on a bench near the door, backs to the wall, looking out of the window onto Main Street. Silver Gulch appeared so quiet it might have been deserted.

As she served them platters of beef, the younger one said, 'Reckon you've a saloon in town that's open?'

'Yes, only the one now. Will you be staying over?'

'Not this trip. We'll be moving on directly.'

A strange answer if they were hunters, but they seemed in no hurry, just sat motionless contemplating the empty street. She brought the pie and coffee and they ate and drank in silence.

When they finished the young man said, 'Fine meal, ma'am. Man named Farnsworth at the saloon?'

'That's right, he owns it. You know him?'

As he paid her, he smiled. 'Oh yes, we know him.'

The older man was standing by the door, watching the empty street, rifle in hand. The younger man said, 'Would appreciate it, ma'am, if you walked along to the saloon with us.'

Mary-Jane was astonished. 'But why? It's no more than a hundred yards. You can't mistake it.'

'None the less, we'd like your company.'

'Well, I suppose I can — there's not likely to be another customer for a while.' She looked more closely at the pair. What was going on here?

'After you,' the young one insisted. He had a slight French accent she noticed now. 'All clear?'

The older man nodded and stepped aside. As they moved along the boardwalk together, the young man gripped her arm.

'You will go in first, if you please,' he told her. 'We'll be close behind you. Don't say anything — we'll do any talking that's necessary.'

'May be won't be necessary at all,'

the man with the rifle said, and hawked in the dust.

Mary-Jane tried to break free. The stranger's grip was hurting, and she had begun to realize what was happening. The young man drew a knife and pricked the back of her neck.

She wished Silver Gulch was not quite so deserted. Alice, where are you? Phil . . . ?

'Don't give us bother and you needn't be hurt,' the young man said. 'Move along easy-like and stay quiet. If Farnsworth sees you, he won't be alarmed.'

Mary-Jane was finding it difficult to get her breath. 'You're going to — ?'

'That's right, ma'am. We're a-goin' to settle an old score.'

★   ★   ★

Across the road, Keyhoe half-dozed in the big armchair Tuttle had loaned him. Patients were in short supply and he might soon have to reconsider his choice of career. He'd drawn a blank last night — losing sleep for nothing — and wondered if there was any point to hunting the ghost again. Maybe the feller had given up. On the other hand, he'd promised Mary-Jane.

The click of boot heels on boardwalk roused him and he glanced through the window. He saw Mary-Jane, accompanied by a stranger and followed by an older man carrying a rifle. She looked pale, unhappy . . . then weak sunlight flashed off the blade of a knife held against her neck.

His heart pounded and he came out of his chair in a hurry, suddenly alert and wondering what the hell was going on. He reached the door and paused, peering through the crack between the door and the frame. He knew he had to avoid alarming the man with the knife. They reached the Five Aces and paused at the batwings.

The young man pushed Mary-Jane forward and got behind her. The older man closed up and raised his big rifle to the firing position.

Now Keyhoe realized they were using her as a shield and the blood froze in his veins. If Farnsworth fired, she could be the first to die.

Suddenly breaking out in a sweat, Keyhoe moved fast, drawing his truncheon as he ran lightly across the road. The attention of the two strangers was concentrated entirely on the saloon. Nearly to the boardwalk, he heard the batwings squeal as they were pushed open.

He shouted desperately, 'Farnsworth, don't shoot! They've got Mary-Jane!'

Ignoring him, the two men pushed her into the saloon and followed her.

* * *

Farnsworth heard the squeal from the door, deliberately not oiled, and glanced casually in the mirror behind the bar. He stiffened at what he glimpsed, whirled about with a gun appearing miraculously in his hand. Then he heard Keyhoe's shout and relaxed pressure on the trigger.

The young man holding a knife at Mary-Jane's throat said venomously, 'Time's up, Farnsworth!'

He recognized the French accent and knew the Marchmont brothers had finally caught up with him. He ducked behind the bar counter.

As the older of the two tracked him with the big buffalo gun, Keyhoe threw a truncheon. It hit the gun arm and the shot went wild and sent the man staggering out from the cover of Mary-Jane.

Farnsworth bared his teeth in a shark's grin and rose and fired his Derringer; the rifle clattered to the floor, followed by a body. One down and one to go, he thought.

'Oh, no,' wailed the younger Marchmont as his brother went down. 'No!' And he hurled the knife.

Farnsworth felt the force of the blow as the knife hit his shoulder, spinning him off-balance. He saw Keyhoe rush in, and Marchmont push Mary-Jane aside and turn to face this new threat, fumbling for a hideout gun.

He ignored the pain in his shoulder and, now with a clear view, shot the other Marchmont in the back with his second barrel.

He leaned back against the wall, awkwardly reloading his twin-barrelled Derringer, thinking; it's over, finally it's ended.

Alice came rushing in, revolver in hand, and looked wildly around. She saw the bodies on the floor and stopped by the batwings. 'What the hell's going on here?' she demanded. Then she saw Mary-Jane shaking in Keyhoe's arms. 'Mary-Jane, what have they done to you?'

'It's just shock,' Keyhoe said. 'She'll be all right in a few minutes.'

'Just shock?' Alice glared at him. 'You bloody men don't realize how fragile we are.'

Farnsworth laughed, and even he could detect a note of hysteria in the sound. 'Fragile? You?'

Tuttle edged cautiously through the batwings into the saloon, shotgun in hand. 'Someone trying to bring back the old days?'

'Just some bodies out of my past,' Farnsworth said. 'It's finished now.' He reached under the counter with his one good hand and lifted high a bottle from his private stock. 'Brandy for the lady. And for me, too, if someone will take this knife out of my shoulder.'

Tuttle said, 'Wait up. I've got bandages in the store,' and went to get them.

Alice poured Mary-Jane a brandy and sat with her, while Keyhoe helped Farnsworth out of his coat and cut away his shirt. When Tuttle returned with bandages, he said, 'Bite down,' and jerked out the knife.

Tuttle washed the wound and made a pad to stem the blood and bandaged him up. 'Going to be sore for a while.'

'Yeah.' Farnsworth grinned palely and splashed brandy into a glass and swallowed it. 'At least I'm here to feel it.' He hefted the Sharps rifle and looked at Keyhoe. 'Lucky for me you were around — that size slug would have made a real mess.'

He shoved the rifle behind the bar as Anson came in and looked warily about him.

'I heard shots — what did I miss?'

'The end of an old story,' Farnsworth said, gesturing at the dead brothers. 'I'm sorry you were involved, Mary-Jane. I suppose I owe you all an explanation, so . . . '

He set up drinks on the house and they gathered in a circle around him.

'The Marchmonts were three brothers working the boats on the Mississippi, as I did myself when younger. Strangely, I seemed to be the only one who'd never heard of them — it turned out later they were notorious.'

He took a sip of brandy. 'I don't suppose you ever saw one of the big side-paddle steamboats?' His eyes misted as if staring into the past. 'Two tall chimneys sticking up by the pilot house, paddle-wheels churning up brown water — the river wasn't called the 'Big Muddy' for nothing; firemen feeding logs into the furnace as fast as they could, the fancy fretwork. And inside, the huge gilt mirrors, a piano tinkling . . . those steamers certainly deserved their nickname of floating palaces.

'I got into a poker game on the upper deck. They were professionals and played me like a sucker, supplying the best champagne. The cards were dealt the way they wanted; all the time it was 'see you, and raise'. The betting went up and up.

'Waal, I caught one of them cheating and challenged him, and he pulled a gun but not fast enough. I beat him to it, and it looked like the other two wanted revenge, but I already had them covered and they hesitated. So I grabbed a handful of money off the table and made a run for it, dived from a paddle-box into the water with the Marchmonts throwing lead after me.'

Farnsworth took another sip of brandy. 'They missed, obviously, but with bullets flying around my head I almost got sucked under a paddle-wheel. That would have been it. I swallowed a mouthful of river and sank, and when I surfaced the steamer had left me behind. I swam to the bank and would have forgotten the whole business, but they hadn't forgotten me. I heard the other two Marchmonts were after me so I moved north out of Louisiana. I kept on the move because, from time to time, I got word they were still hunting me.'

He shook his head, as if wondering why they had bothered. 'I finally ended up here because, by chance, I got saddled with this saloon and couldn't sell it. At least, now, I won't be constantly looking over my shoulder any more, and that's some relief.'

Keyhoe had listened fascinated, and now he regarded the two bodies on the floor and turned to Anson. 'What will the law have to say about this?'

The lawyer brought out a handkerchief and polished his spectacles.

'The law, Mr Keyhoe?' Anson smiled. 'You're not back east now. It's maybe forty miles to the nearest law office and if you reported this the sheriff would probably think you crazy.'

'If someone will give me a hand,' Farnsworth said, 'I'll drop these two down one of the old mine shafts. It's the law of the gun here, Mr Keyhoe. That's all we have.'

'It'll be my pleasure,' Alice said, and started to drag one of the bodies outside by the boots.

Despite her protests, Keyhoe insisted on escorting Mary-Jane back to her restaurant.

'I'm over it now,' she said. 'I admit I was upset at first — thought I might be joining Riley if there is anywhere we go.' She tried a weak smile.

They walked along the boardwalk together and Keyhoe opened the door and paused. He caught a strong smell of fish.

An old man sprouting grey whiskers and smoking a pipe sat at a table; he wore big boots and his clothing was ragged and dusty.

'Hi, Mary-Jane, wondered where you'd got to. I came down 'cause I got tired of eating fish. Could do with a steak — brought yuh some fresh-caught trout.'

Keyhoe relaxed. Despite his appearance, the pipe-smoker was obviously an old friend.

'Hi, Virgil,' she said, 'one steak coming up. Some of my customers are tired of steak all the time, so you're more than welcome.'

She indicated her companion. 'This is Phil Keyhoe, he's a dentist. Phil, sit and talk with Virgil; he's been prospecting higher up the gulch.'

As she vanished into the kitchen, Keyhoe sat, and asked, 'Is there really the chance of a new strike?'

Virgil puffed on his pipe producing a cloud of smoke that reminded Keyhoe of a bonfire. 'Always a chance where there's been one somewhere nearby. It happens a vein can break and start again someplace else. It's a chance, no more — but a chance is enough for any real prospector.'

A delicious smell came from the kitchen and Keyhoe's mouth watered.

Virgil said, 'I'm one of the few still looking. Some folk give up too easy and that's stupid.'

'But nothing so far?'

'Nothing.' Virgil had a twinkle in his eyes as he asked, 'How's the tooth racket? Mary-Jane's look okay to me.'

'Mary-Jane's are excellent,' Keyhoe replied gravely.

She came from the kitchen with Virgil's steak, and two plates of fish.

'I wish you'd try to get down more often, Virgil. When the boom was on, I had hunters bringing in deer from the hills. Now it's nothing but beef, beef, beef.'

Virgil didn't reply; he'd put down his pipe and was busy enjoying his steak.

# 7

Keyhoe had a mental map of the layout of the old mining area and the place where he'd lost the ghost on a previous occasion. Just opposite was a rock shelter where someone had started to tunnel into the face of the gulch. It provided cover and he was in shadow.

He took his position early so he was sure of his location. The night was quiet except for a trickle of water somewhere. Something else to check out, but not right now. He settled to wait.

There was no cloud and the stars were hard and bright. He wouldn't lose the ghost this time, if he showed up. Waiting in the cold he began to go numb, and dreamed of Mary-Jane. Every few minutes, he massaged his legs to keep the blood flowing.

And then a shadow moved. Keyhoe tensed, it had to be ... he rushed forward, eager. You won't get away this time, he thought.

A gunshot echoed off rock walls. Flame stabbed the night air. A bullet whined past his left ear and, cursing, he dropped flat on the ground. Another shot. Close, but no prize. He crawled sideways to get behind a chunk of discarded timber. A third shot, and splinters flew into his face.

He crawled further in the dark to get behind metal. A bullet spanged off rusting iron. He waited, holding his breath.

The silence stretched. Was the gunman waiting for him to move? Who was it shooting at him? There had been no sign of the ghost this time, just an unknown gunman. Because he was hunting the ghost? Or because of Mary-Jane?

He waited patiently, listening; and imagined his attacker doing the same. He felt in the dirt for a pebble and tossed it away from him. It made a small sound but no shot followed.

Cautiously, he peered over the top of his metal shield and saw no hint of movement.

He was beginning to freeze and knew he'd have to shift soon. Perhaps the unknown man was already in the warm, laughing. Keyhoe took the risk and rose to his full height, ready to duck if he glimpsed red flame. Nothing happened; it seemed his attacker had gone.

Keeping in shadow, he withdrew silently to the alley-way and then to Main Street. There was no light in Alice's shop but, across the starlit expanse of dust, an oil lamp glimmered in the general store. Keyhoe moved quickly across the street and pushed open the door.

Tuttle was sitting by the stove, mug of coffee in hand. 'Sounded like someone shooting. Again. Town's getting real lively.'

'Shooting at me. I was hoping to catch the so-called ghost.'

'Looks like he missed,' Tuttle said, and added, 'Ghosts don't fire guns.'

'I agree. I need a gun if someone's going to take pot-shots at me.'

'Sounds reasonable. What kind do you fancy?'

'A shotgun, and I'd like extra shells.'

'Interesting choice — it's what I favour myself. Used one before?'

Keyhoe nodded, reluctant to admit he'd used one against the gangs on the streets of New York. It was a weapon even they respected.

Tuttle gave him a sharp look, got out of his chair and went into the back room. Keyhoe looked casually about the store, noted an open sack half-filled with white powder. Flour?

Before he could check, Tuttle returned with the gun he'd carried into the Five Aces.

Keyhoe looked it over, a double-barrelled gun, well-worn. He broke it open and looked down the barrels; spotless. The stock was smooth, the metalwork oiled. Someone had taken care of this weapon.

'Your own?'

'It is now.' Tuttle's face crinkled. 'It was my father's.'

He went behind the counter and opened a drawer, spilled a handful of shells onto the wooden top.

'It came in handy when this was a boom-town. All kinds of desperadoes flocked here and reckoned they could help themselves to whatever they wanted.'

'How much?' Keyhoe asked.

'You can pay me for the shells. The gun you're only borrowing — ghosts are bad for business. You'll take coffee?'

Keyhoe loaded the gun and sat easy.

* * *

Hugo Bishop arrived in town looking like a storm-cloud, his mouth a grim slit and a frown darkening his face. Mary-Jane was an important part of Silver Gulch, and Silver Gulch, he reckoned, was his.

It was the money he paid his loggers that kept Tuttle in business, and the saloon, and — yes — Mary-Jane's restaurant. His was the only money-making business around and that, in his opinion, meant he owned the town. He ignored Cade; the Bar C was barely surviving.

And now someone had dared to threaten the woman he intended, eventually, to marry. If it hadn't been for Farnsworth and that dentist feller, she might have been hurt. He hated to admit they were due thanks.

He knew not everyone saw it his way, yet, but they would. Gregson, following behind as he strode along the board-walk knew enough to keep quiet and touch his hat when he got an order. It amused Bishop that, at this moment, Gregson seemed wary of his mood.

He reached the restaurant, pushed open the door and swaggered in. Mary-Jane sat at a table with an old man smoking a pipe, drinking coffee and chatting. Their conversation stopped abruptly at his entrance.

She looked hot and sweaty from the

kitchen, her face flushed. He was disappointed that she did not appear glad to see him.

'I heard about it, Mary-Jane,' he boomed, 'and I can't allow you to live here on your own any longer. It's far too dangerous — obviously, there's no telling who might walk in. Or what they might do.'

A gleam came to her eyes and she tossed her red hair back. 'Dangerous? I'll tell you who's in danger.' She picked up a kitchen knife from the table and pointed it at him. 'The next stranger who walks in here — and the next man who upsets me.'

She took a deep breath. 'I don't mind admitting, now, that I was scared. But it won't happen again. Anyone who even looks threatening had better run for cover, 'cause I'm seriously angry.'

She waved the knife under his nose for emphasis, and Bishop was momentarily taken aback.

'Yes, well, quite . . . I've decided to leave Gregson here to make sure no one bothers you — '

'Gregson!' She saw the logger smirk, and almost spat the name. 'If he tries anything again, I'll spit and roast him for supper!'

The old man removed the pipe from his mouth to show a few stained teeth in a grin. 'And I'll jump at the chance to help her.'

'Again?' Bishop picked up her meaning and swung around to glare at his logger. 'What's been going on behind my back?'

Gregson took a pace backwards, mumbling, 'Aw, it was nothing, boss. I had a drink too many and forgot myself, is all. No harm done.'

'Is that so? We'll discuss this later. Mary-Jane, I accept that you don't want Gregson around, so you'll stay at my house. It's big and comfortable and you'll have a room to yourself. You won't need to cook any more so — '

The old man laughed out loud. Mary-Jane stared. She remembered Alice's words and took a long breath.

'If you think ... I can look after myself, and there's people here I trust if I need help. So there's nothing doing. You keep your distance, Mr Bishop.'

★ ★ ★

Keyhoe carried the shotgun, loaded and ready for instant action, even though he didn't anticipate an attack during daylight hours. As he toured North End, looking for any sign the gunman may have left, the sun was shining and beginning to warm the air. He went from shack to shack, peering inside before moving on.

Ever alert, he was taken by surprise when a soft voice called, 'Here.'

He turned sharply. Wu stood in an open doorway, beckoning him. 'Here is where the ghost goes to earth.'

Keyhoe went forward warily. He'd saved the Chinese from the Texans, after all, and there seemed no need to fear him, but he hadn't heard the door open.

'That's what I'm looking for — how he does his disappearing act.'

Wu retreated inside the shack and Keyhoe followed him. Bare wood walls, bits of shelving, dirty windows; but not enough dust on the floor to reveal footprints.

The small Chinese man pointed to a loose floor-board, and Keyhoe shifted it. Below was an opening, and a wooden ladder leading down into darkness. There was an unpleasant smell of damp.

'Easy to get lost down there,' Wu said cheerfully. 'Many tunnels, go this-a-way.' He gestured vigorously.

'How come you know so much about it?'

'Before the silver ends, I work down there. A miner.'

Keyhoe replaced the plank carefully. He didn't want to warn whoever was playing ghost that his secret was no longer a secret. He intended to be waiting for him that night, and however many nights it took.

'Strange place to dig a hole,' he said.

Wu smiled. 'Not so strange. Shaft was part of the mine first. Then, when no longer used, shack was built over, and forgotten.'

Except by someone who enjoys scaring women, Keyhoe thought. He inspected the door of the shack; it swung silently to and fro on well-oiled hinges.

Yeah, real handy for anyone wanting to play ghost.

# 8

Keyhoe was working in his office, bearing down on the patient in the chair; Owen, one of Cade's cowhands. He was concentrating so he was only vaguely aware of a wagon passing on Main Street and a lot of shouting.

He didn't pay much attention because he had a knee on Owen's stomach to hold him down and the forceps groping for a tooth.

'Never mind the excitement — keep your head still and your mouth wide.'

Finally he obtained a good purchase on the aching molar and eased it out. 'That's got it. Finish your whiskey and rinse out your mouth.'

Keyhoe cleaned up after inserting a cotton-wool plug, then went to the door and looked down the dusty street. The wagon had stopped near Mary-Jane's restaurant and the volume of sound suggested that something violent might be happening.

He frowned. 'Any of your outfit in town?'

The Texan, trying to relax, mumbled, 'Only Eddie, he's getting a meal at Mary-Jane's. The kid's kinda sweet on her.'

'Is there anyone who isn't?' Keyhoe picked up his shotgun, checked it was loaded and went to the door. 'Looks like Eddie's in trouble.'

He crossed the street and took deliberate strides along the boardwalk. A crowd of loggers were obviously stirred up about something.

He saw Gregson to the front, urging them on. 'String him up,' he was bawling.

Keyhoe felt his flesh crawl. He'd once seen a mob in action, and nothing could have stopped them. This crowd was subtly different. The men were obviously liquored up, their faces flushed. It was an excited crowd, potentially dangerous with Gregson encouraging them. But he detected no blood lust among the men.

There was plenty of shouting, and some laughter, but it seemed a cold-blooded affair, and Keyhoe wondered exactly how this had started.

'Hang him high!' That was Gregson again.

Keyhoe looked carefully but could see no sign of Bishop. He reached the edge of the crowd and used his weight to push through to the doorway. A couple of burly loggers were trying to drag Eddie outside, with the cowboy struggling ineffectually. Behind them, Mary-Jane and Virgil were protesting, hanging on to one of the loggers.

'Get away, woman,' Gregson shouted.

The old prospector had no chance against big lumbermen with plenty of muscle; he went down.

'Cowards,' Mary-Jane shouted. 'Leave him alone.'

She looked around desperately for help, and saw Keyhoe. 'Phil,' she called. 'Save Eddie, please. I know he hasn't done anything wrong.'

The loggers had the cowboy almost through the doorway, and Gregson was putting the noose in a hemp rope about his neck. 'Say your prayers, cowboy.'

Keyhoe brought up his shotgun and said, loudly: 'Let him go. Both barrels are loaded, and I'll gut-shoot a couple of you if you don't release him immediately.'

Gregson swore and turned on him. 'Keep outa this — Eddie's been playing ghost and scaring folk, and we're goin' to stop him. Permanently. Interfere, and you'll buy into trouble.'

'Yeah,' someone in the crowd shouted, 'haul him up!'

Keyhoe pushed forward, swinging the muzzle of the shotgun up to cover Gregson. He jammed both barrels into the logger's stomach. 'You first, Gregson, unless you let Eddie go.'

Gregson glared at him, uncertain. Then from across the street came the crack of a rifle and a bullet lifted the logger's hat from his head. A muffled voice said, 'Let him go, or I'll pump some serious lead your way.'

Owen was taking a hand.

'Me too!' Alice came striding across the road, revolver in hand. 'This is your last chance.'

Reluctantly the timbermen edged back and Eddie threw off the noose.

Owen said, 'Get on your horse, Eddie, and ride back to the ranch, pronto.'

'I haven't finished my meal yet — '

'Do as I say,' Owen yelled. 'Get back and report to Mr Cade. Now!'

It seemed the simple-minded cowboy didn't grasp the seriousness of his situation, but he moved towards his horse, unhitched and mounted. He waved to Mary-Jane and trotted out of town.

Keyhoe looked at Gregson. 'That didn't hurt a bit, did it? Whatever made you think Eddie was our ghost? Does Mr Bishop know about this?'

Gregson turned away, white with fury and shaking; as if he didn't trust himself to speak, but his expression was savage. He walked quickly towards the wagon. His gang of loggers sobered up fast.

As he climbed up to the driver's seat, Gregson shouted, 'You won't get away with this — wait'll I tell Mr Bishop. I'll be back when you're on your own.'

Alice snorted. 'Just make sure you're on your own — or I'll be taking a hand.'

Keyhoe lowered his gun as the wagon trundled away. He stepped inside the restaurant to see Mary-Jane bathing a cut over Virgil's eye.

'It ain't nothin',' the old man muttered as he filled his pipe.

Alice said, 'You sure do attract trouble, Mary-Jane.'

'Thanks, both of you,' she said. 'You too, Virgil. I know Eddie does silly things, but there's no real harm in him.'

'I don't reckon he's the one playing ghost.' Keyhoe looked out of the window and saw Owen swing into the saddle and gallop after Eddie.

'I wonder what that was all about?' he mused aloud, and shrugged. 'A bit of excitement sure works up an appetite.'

Mary-Jane smiled. 'Well, that is something I can remedy.'

★   ★   ★

Anson offered to buy Keyhoe a drink and, to be sociable, he accepted. Farnsworth joined them at their table, idly shuffling a pack of cards one-handed and laying them down. He seemed altogether more relaxed.

'With this shoulder so stiff,' he explained, 'I need the practice.'

Anson sipped cautiously at a whiskey as if afraid it might affect his judgement. 'A fine thing,' he said, 'you saving Eddie. I'm afraid I was keeping my head down.' He paused. 'This will probably be my last visit. I'm going back when the coach calls next. Those that will sell, have sold. Those that won't — '

'Like me,' Farnsworth said, 'and Mary-Jane, and one or two others.'

'Stubborn as a Mexican mule,' the

lawyer agreed with a smile.

'But why?' Keyhoe asked.

'Waal, let's put it this way.' Farnsworth casually turned up four cards he'd dealt to himself; all four were aces. 'Both Cade and Bishop were doing well when Silver Gulch was booming. Meat and timber were in demand — today, they're still selling, but only a fraction of the business they did before.'

He dealt another hand. 'Neither look as if they're thinking of leaving and I wonder sometimes, in the dark of the night, what it is they know that I don't.'

'It's a good point,' Keyhoe said. 'Does Tuttle feel the same way?'

'I suspect he might.'

Keyhoe glanced sideways at the lawyer. 'Mr Anson, you must have wondered at some time if your client and the ghost have any connection.'

'Of course I have. Strictly speaking, any knowledge of my client is confidential . . . However, it is obvious that whoever is frightening away people has local information. My client is not local, but based in Washington. A lawyer, like myself.'

Farnsworth glanced upwards as a drumming sounded overhead. 'Here it comes — rain at last. Cade will be pleased — grass and water for his animals.'

# 9

The rain came down heavily for a while so Keyhoe waited it out in the saloon, absently chewing on a tooth-pick.

'Phil', Mary-Jane had called him, and that was satisfying; but it wasn't the living rivals who concerned him as much as a dead one. The ghost had to be caught and shown up.

Looking past the batwings was like staring at a grey curtain. It grew dark early and Farnsworth lit an oil lamp. Anson stared out at the rain with a glum expression. Talk died away.

When the rain eased off, Keyhoe moved quickly along the boardwalk to the store. Already the thick dust of Main Street was turning to mud.

Tuttle was alone, sitting by his pot-bellied stove. He poured coffee into a mug and handed it to him as if this was an automatic action. Perhaps he did this for every potential customer. Perhaps he just wanted company and a good gossip.

'What can I do for you today, Mr Keyhoe?'

'I need matches and a candle.'

The storekeeper almost smiled. 'Hope you're not going to start a fire.'

'Nothing like that. I want to take a look at the bottom of one of the old mine shafts.'

'Candles are not a good idea. Gases accumulate. I've got something better if you wait a minute.' Tuttle went into his back room and returned with an enclosed lantern. 'Oil lasts longer. I keep it filled for emergencies.'

From below the counter he brought some matches and demonstrated how to light it.

'Let me have it back when you've finished with it — and don't get to exploring down any of the tunnels. That can be dangerous.'

Keyhoe drained his coffee, thanked him and left. As evening closed in the rain stopped, though the sky remained banked with dark clouds. He waited till the light had almost gone, then eased quietly along the back alley with shotgun and lantern. The mud, he discovered, slowed him down.

He cautiously approached the shack where Wu had shown him a ladder leading down, keeping in shadow and avoiding any obstacle that might make a noise. He remembered the oiled hinges and reminded himself of the need to stay alert; there would be no squeak from rusting metal to warn him the ghost was about. And he was determined the person responsible should not escape him this time.

He found fresh cover with a clear view of the door — not that he could see much because cloud mostly obscured the stars. The air felt chill and damp.

Somewhere higher up the gulch he heard the scream of a victim as a predator pounced. He bared his teeth, because that was exactly how he felt — waiting for his prey to reveal itself.

He tucked his hands under his armpits. Occasionally the moon managed to show a pale light through a break in the cloud layer. Then he saw the door swing silently open and a white figure appear.

Keyhoe unfroze and moved forward, bringing his shotgun up to a firing position.

'Hold it right there, feller — or I'll blast yuh to Kingdom Come!'

The figure vanished and Keyhoe squeezed a trigger, firing one barrel. Obviously whoever it was had whitened only one side of his disguise; so the ghost had only to turn away to disappear.

Keyhoe swore, picked up his lantern and ran forward. He reached the hut, the door still swinging, and peered inside. The hut was empty, the plank removed and a hole showing. He walked in warily and stared down into darkness, hearing movement but seeing nothing.

He fumbled for a match and struck it, lit the wick. He held the lamp over the hole but could still see no one below, and sounds of movement were fading. He went down the ladder and touched bottom, lifting the lamp high to look about him.

The ground was uneven. The rock walls were damp and the roof supported by timber props. He started forward, intent only on catching the ghost, and went on till the tunnel forked. He paused there.

Left or right? He listened, but heard nothing to help him decide which way his quarry had gone. He tossed a mental coin and went down the left-hand tunnel, hoping he'd guessed correctly.

He had not gone many paces when he heard the creak of timber shifting. Behind him. He turned, raising the lantern and caught a glimpse of the ghost wrenching at one of the props holding up the roof . . . then a fall of dust hid the figure.

Keyhoe ran forward, too late. He heard a chuckle, a muffled half-familiar voice: 'Goodbye, Mister Dentist!' The ghost vanished as rocks fell, blocking the tunnel.

Keyhoe realized the left-hand turn had been the wrong choice, and remembered Tuttle's words: 'Don't get to exploring down any of the tunnels. That can be dangerous.' Ruefully, he had to admit the correctness of the warning; he shouldn't have let his eagerness to catch the ghost override caution.

The rumble of falling rock seemed to go on and on for ever and he began to wonder if he would be able to claw his way through.

Eventually silence came and the dust began to settle. He placed his lantern on the ground and started to remove the nearest rocks — and soon found it to be a losing battle; as he removed one, two fell. The more he removed, the more fell. Many more. So far he seemed only to be making his situation worse and, with a sigh, he paused to take stock.

★　★　★

Tuttle heard the rain drumming again on the roof. Apparently the lull had been temporary; and, judging by the ache in his joints, this time it had come to stay.

He put more wood on the stove, lit a lamp and refilled his coffee pot.

The sound made him remember his wife; she had always liked rain, said it freshened the air. True enough, but it also turned Main Street to a sea of mud. Which meant no customers. Sometimes he wondered why he bothered to stay open at all.

Years had passed and he was beginning to feel old; he opened and reread the last letter from his daughter in California, urging him to retire and live with them.

California sounded right well for youngsters starting out, but what would he retire to? He'd always worked in a general store, first back east and then, as the frontier shifted, further west with each move till his daughter married and his wife died.

He didn't feel like moving again; the incentive had gone, and he was a creature of habit, reluctant to change. And he was curious to know who was playing ghost and who Anson was buying town lots for.

He considered Farnsworth, and Bishop and Cade, each apparently unwilling to leave Silver Gulch. Of course, there was also Mary-Jane; all three were sniffing at her heels like hound dogs after a bitch. There was Alice, too.

And now there was the dentist, Keyhoe, a human catalyst if ever there was one. His wife had always fancied herself as a match-maker and he had no doubt she would already have been at work matching Mary-Jane and Keyhoe. He smiled at the thought.

It seemed obvious the newcomer hadn't always been a dentist. The way he'd stood up for Wu and Eddie said a lot about his character; as well as the determination he was showing in going after the ghost.

Tuttle had a feeling that interesting

things were about to happen. He looked out at the rain and took the coffee off the stove and put a frying pan on; time for a fry-up.

★　★　★

Keyhoe, buried alive, thought of the miners who hadn't made it back to the surface. If they hadn't, what chance had he? He imagined there must be other entrances, so there must be other exits too, but would the oil in his lamp last long enough to find one?

He smiled a trifle grimly; there was only one way to find out. He tucked the shotgun under his arm, picked up the lantern and turned his back on the pile of rubble.

He thought briefly of Mary-Jane as he plodded along; would he ever see her again? The uneven ground made walking difficult, and he had to duck his head wherever the roof sagged. He came to another fall, but this one was easy to climb over and he continued.

Some of the pit props were rotting in places and gave him an uneasy feeling.

He could hear, faintly, a trickle of water someplace. An underground river? He hurried then, but the sound gradually faded away.

The air began to taste funny, and he paused, sniffing warily. Gas building up? There was nothing he could do about that but keep moving and hope it wasn't serious.

The tunnel divided again. Keep going left, he decided; at least he'd have a system if it became necessary to retrace his steps. Further on, the tunnel divided again, and again he turned left. By now, he imagined, he must be under the mountains.

Water trickled from a crack in the rock, and he cupped his hands and drank. It was ice cold and refreshing. Pieces of loose rock fell away and he stepped back hurriedly. It was then that he realized he'd left the old silver mine; there were no longer any pit props to support the roof.

Somewhere along the way he'd entered a natural fault in the rock, or one that had been carved by a torrent of water.

Bits of debris continued to fall and he helped, making a hole big enough to climb through. But would that get him anywhere? He had almost decided not to bother when he became aware of a smell from beyond. He lifted his lantern higher . . .

\* \* \*

Virgil, an experienced prospector, knew how to look out for himself in bad weather. He had sound boots that kept his feet dry, a slicker and a hat; and he kept under the thickly clad branches of trees as he climbed the mud trail towards the mountains, so he caught only a few drips.

The cut over his eye had healed and his head no longer ached, but that didn't mean he was going to hang around Silver Gulch. Enough was enough. Virgil was a loner who preferred a quiet life; he figured bears and wolves were a lot less violent than his own kind.

He often dreamed of Mary-Jane, so it had been pleasant to see her again and get a decent cooked meal; and he had cold cuts in his pack, enough for several days.

He bypassed Bishop's fort-like house and kept going. A lamp burned there, meaning someone was home, but he'd had enough of lynchers. Crazy men. Why they'd decided to string up Eddie he couldn't fathom, and he wasn't about to ask.

He plodded steadily higher. He knew of a dry place where he could wait out the storm; a place nobody else knew. And sometimes heavy rain washed something interesting to the surface; he reckoned it was about time his luck changed — maybe this trip.

Still climbing under the trees, Virgil watched a deluge run downhill and recalled, it was a night like this when the mine flooded and Mary-Jane's husband died. Waal, now, it didn't matter because there was no one down there any more.

★   ★   ★

Keyhoe saw the scattered remains of human bodies, and guessed he'd found the miners trapped in the fall. Obviously, they too had been searching for another way out and this was as far as they'd got.

He hesitated, then climbed through the gap. Even if he'd known any of them in life they wouldn't have been recognizable in death.

Clothes had disintegrated, there was rusting metal; odd bits of leather looked as if it had been chewed . . . rats? Down here? That gave him a bad feeling and he lifted his lamp higher.

Bones lay scattered at random, some jumbled together. He saw a helmet half-off a skull and removed it to wear himself; it might save him a few knocks in low places. It was a difficult situation to read.

Some bones lay over others as they sprawled here and there. Crushed fingers grasped an ankle bone. Had they been trying to escape something? Helping each other? Fighting?

He remembered his own initial panic, the feeling of being shut in with a weight of rock overhead. Anything might have happened after their last lamp failed.

He counted the bodies: seven, and murmured a brief prayer over them. About to turn away, the light from his lamp caught the gleam of a gold ring encircling a bony finger. Not one of the other bodies wore a ring, so there was a better than even chance he had stumbled across Mary-Jane's husband.

He bent over and removed the ring and slipped it in his pocket. Now he could confirm that her husband was truly dead and the ghost a cruel fake. If he could get out.

He withdrew hurriedly when he

noticed a threatening bulge in the roof. Barely had he returned to the tunnel when more rock fell, reburying the bodies.

He turned his back and set off again. He had not gone far when the lantern began to fail. It spluttered several times and he hurried along. As the last of the oil burned away, the light went out. Darkness closed about him like a shroud

★　★　★

Wu had been hiding in one of the old cabins when his big friend challenged the ghost. He often used one of the derelict buildings in North End, and it was rare for anybody to bother him there.

He saw the ghost vanish into his shack, closely followed by Keyhoe, and waited patiently for the outcome; the Chinese man had a lot of patience. Neither reappeared. He watched the rain come down in sheets.

It was obvious the big man knew nothing about mines, but Wu did. He'd worked down there before it closed, and knew it was likely to flood. Because Keyhoe had saved his pigtail, he felt obligated.

Making up his mind, he waited for a lull in the downpour and plodded through the mud to the shack. Inside, the plank was still up. No light or sound came from below. He went nimbly down the ladder and edged forward till he found the rockfall. Now he knew why Keyhoe had not returned. There was no sign of the ghost, who obviously knew of another exit.

Wu went up top again and peered out at the rain, troubled and wondering what was best to do. If he went for help, who would believe him? Mary-Jane would; he often got left-overs from the restaurant woman, and liked her. Alice might; despite her apparent hatred of men, she sometimes gave him a stale loaf.

But none of them knew the workings

as well as he did. There was one, of course; perhaps he should tell Keyhoe about that one? If he survived.

The rain was coming down even harder and it didn't look like stopping. That meant . . . he remembered a place where water ran out; only a trickle, but the crack could be widened, letting out more water. Yes, that should help, so that's what he would do.

He needed a pickaxe. There were plenty of those lying around and he searched, discarding one after another until he found one that satisfied him.

He walked through the rain till he came to the part of the gulch he remembered and looked around. There was little light and the giant trees made deep shadows; the drumbeat of heavy rain blotted out the faint trickle he ought to hear where water escaped from the rock face.

He cast about, searching — he knew it was somewhere nearby — when a dark and shaggy shape erupted from the darkest shadows. It roared a challenge and Wu turned and ran.

The shape came lumbering after him and, glancing back, he realized he had disturbed a bear. He crashed through the undergrowth, stumbling in a panic; he had once seen what a grizzly did to a man it caught. He blanked the image from his mind.

The bear dropped to all fours, sniffing his scent as it followed.

Wu, desperate now, turned and flung the pickaxe at his pursuer. The bear roared as the pick struck its nose. It bellowed angrily and turned on the pick. Wu kept going, as though Indians were after his scalp.

★ ★ ★

Keyhoe stood absolutely still in the dark, smelling the sooty wick. This wasn't ordinary darkness; it was utter blackness, as if he'd suddenly been struck blind. There was not a glimmer, not a gleam of light anywhere.

For a moment, panic threatened to

overwhelm him, but he knew he had to resist that at any cost. He took a deep breath and forced himself to breathe out slowly in a controlled manner. He took a second breath, and a third. Gradually the panic subsided.

He fumbled a match from his pocket and struck it to realign himself. He reached out to touch the left-hand wall before the match burned away.

Utter blackness descended again, but he was able to move forward, following the left-hand wall and bearing left all the time. He must get somewhere eventually; he could not afford to doubt the existence of another exit.

Somewhere. He shuffled along, stumbling on the unevenness. The wall was rough and took the skin off his fingertips, and slippery with dampness; but he was determined not to strike another match until he had to.

He felt his way along by touch, pausing occasionally to listen. There was the sound of running water in the background; then it was dripping from the roof onto his helmet. At least he wouldn't go thirsty.

The ground fell away and he stumbled into a shallow hole, climbed out, sweating. It could have been an abyss . . .

Soon he realized he was splashing through ankle-deep water. Must be raining outside, he thought. The idea did nothing to cheer him, but brought to mind the bodies of the miners he'd found.

He plodded on, the water rising steadily, swirling about his calves, and moving faster. His feet were numb with cold. The water must run out somewhere, he told himself, and kept going.

Presently the water was up to his waist and he struggled not to lose his footing and be swept away. He paused to strike a match, but the brief light revealed only the jagged walls of the tunnel going on and on and the dark water trying to sweep him away.

The gallery sloped down and he banged his helmet on a projecting crag;

despite this protection, the blow half-stunned him. He submerged and had to make extra effort to bring his nose and mouth up to breathe air. The water was running faster, pushing him along, the level rising all the time.

He went on because there was nothing else he could do. He felt isolated as never before, closed about by blackness, freezing as the water rose to chest level. The roof seemed to press lower and there was still no hint of an opening to the outside world. The end seemed inevitable.

# 10

Tuttle sat with Anson, sipping coffee by the wood stove in the general store. He thought the lawyer seemed depressed as they watched the rain; it seemed to have settled in for a long spell and was coming down heavily. Anson looked at his watch and frowned.

'Reckon he'll make it?'

'Surely. Wallace is an old-timer. Prides himself on getting the stage through, no matter what. Might be a bit late, due to the trail turning to mud . . . can't see much point these days, stopping off at what amounts to a ghost town. There's no use us pretending it's not.'

Tuttle watched with sharp eyes but Anson didn't rise to the bait. He had been hoping for a clue to the client buying up town lots.

Anson said stiffly, 'Some of us have

business to attend to.'

Tuttle inclined his head, listening. He could hear the stagecoach now, the driver whipping his horses along and cursing the weather. The coach rattled along Main Street, rain drumming a tattoo on its roof. When it stopped outside, Anson rose to his feet.

'Thanks for the coffee,' he said, and hurried to get inside the coach.

'Any time,' Tuttle muttered, his attention entirely on the arriving passenger who stepped down into the mud with a small case.

'Bring the others, will you, driver?'

The new arrival struggled up onto the boardwalk and into the store. He looked about him with a doubtful expression as Wallace came in and dumped two large and heavy bags.

'Are you sure this is the right place? I expected a proper town and a first class hotel.'

Strange accent, Tuttle thought, not a Westerner, and his gaze sharpened.

The newcomer offered the driver a

tip. Wallace ignored it, spat through the doorway and said, 'I'm off.' He went out into the downpour as if glad to escape.

His passenger wore good-quality clothes of a strange cut, gloves, and carried a cane. He removed his Derby to reveal blond hair cropped short.

The storekeeper filled another mug from the pot on the stove and offered it.

'Take coffee with me, stranger? My name's Tuttle. I run this store and I'm still the mayor of Silver Gulch until they get around to another election. Not sure when that'll be.'

'Thank you. A hot drink will be appreciated. And some information.'

'You a city gent? A bit off your course, aren't you?'

'Not if this is Silver Gulch. I have a business interest here.'

Tuttle confirmed that it was, and eyed the newcomer's expensive outfit as he struggled to remove thin shoes plastered with thick mud. Youngish, and handsome in a way. He supposed this was one of those Eastern dudes he'd heard about.

'Figure maybe you come from New York?'

'Actually, through New York and, more recently, Washington. It was there I heard about this place — thought I'd get in on the ground floor, you know.'

Tuttle wondered what it was he was supposed to know, but persisted. 'It's your accent — I can't rightly place that at all.'

'Ah, I'm English, from across the Atlantic. You've heard of England.'

'Heard of it,' Tuttle admitted.

'Strong coffee,' his visitor said, putting down the empty mug. 'My name is Sinclair, by the way. Now, can you direct me to the nearest hotel? I assume it will have a restaurant and all the usual facilities?'

Tuttle allowed himself a small smile.

'Not quite, Mr Sinclair. Town's more or less shut down since the silver gave out. Hotel too, but I can give you a key. Room with a bed, a dollar a night. No room service — the building right across the street.'

Sinclair looked amazed. 'Shut down?'

'Yep, you can get a meal at Mary-Jane's, right along the boardwalk. Only place left open.'

Sinclair went to the door and stared out at the rain. 'I don't think I'm in that much of a hurry. Can I leave my bags here while I get something to eat?'

Tuttle nodded, and Sinclair opened an umbrella and made a dash along the plank-walk.

Wu ran as if chased by a Chinese devil, bouncing off trees and crashing through undergrowth. He sounded like an army regiment blundering about in a cannonade. He hardly felt the rain lashing down, so sure was he the bear was breathing down his neck, reaching out with its great claws to savage him. He slid and slithered down hill in the mud, gasping for air. He hadn't run like this, not even with cowboys after his pigtail.

So when another figure loomed up in

front of him, he nearly had a heart attack as he skidded to a halt.

A voice said, 'What are you up to, Wu? You're scaring the game for miles around.'

Wu peered forward. It was Eddie standing there in the wet, holding a rifle.

'Bear,' he gasped out. 'Right behind me.'

Eddie peered into the gloom between the trees. 'There's nothing behind you — you must have imagined it.'

'No, not imagine. Real bear. Big bear, all dark fur and teeth and claws — '

'Show me where you saw it.'

'Not me. Go back to hut quick, and hide.'

Eddie gestured with his rifle. 'C'mon, Wu, no bear's goin' to chase you, all the noise you were making. Just show me where you saw it. I'm after shooting a bear to make a rug for Mary-Jane.'

Wu stared at him. Only Eddie could think of hunting a bear in pouring rain, but nothing much bothered him since his accident. He suspected that part of the cowboy's brain had switched off.

He'd suddenly got the idea of hunting a grizzly and that's what he was doing. Once Eddie got an idea into his head, he stuck to it, no matter what. It filled his head till there was no room for anything else. Eddie was a one idea at a time man.

Now he said, 'C'mon, Wu, Mary-Jane feeds you, doesn't she? This is your chance to do something for her. Winter's coming and a fur rug is a good thing to have.'

'Okay, but you shoot bear first.'

'Sure thing.'

Wu slowly retraced his steps, freezing each time a twig snapped or a leaf, bowed by a weight of water, poured an icy stream down his neck. Moving shadows unnerved him and he went back uphill reluctantly.

Eventually he came across his pick-axe, and the handle showed teeth marks.

'Guess you were right,' Eddie said.

Wu picked it up to use as a weapon and moved even more slowly as he headed for the place where water trickled down the face of the gulch. 'Here,' he said, 'this is where I first saw the bear.'

Eddie sniffed the air and pushed aside the undergrowth, following the path the animal had made. He disappeared in a curtain of rain.

Wu hesitated. True, Eddie had a rifle, but he was looking for the bear. Now was the time to sneak back to his shack hide-away . . .

He remembered Keyhoe somewhere underground with the water rising. He looked around quickly to make sure the bear had not returned.

Then he swung his pick to loosen pieces of rock, and kept chipping away. Gradually the trickle of water became a flow, followed by a sudden outpour. He swung the pick with all his strength and a solid mass of rock fell away, almost burying him.

The outpour became a flood, drenching him, and he backed away. The water level would go down now.

★ ★ ★

Mary-Jane put another log in the stove and listened to the rain on the roof. She'd heard the stagecoach arrive and depart and wondered if there might be a customer. Now that Virgil had left she was tempted to close the restaurant early.

She hated rain. It was rain that had flooded the mine and brought down the roof, killing her husband along with half a dozen others. That had been a bad time, a time when she had resolutely refused to believe that Riley wasn't coming back.

Riley, with his Irish blarney, his 'Darling, when did I last tell yuh you get more beautiful every day?' and his cajoling 'Love yuh, honey' when he wanted something. Riley, with the lilt in his voice, the smiling eyes and caring ways. Riley, whistling while he chopped wood. Yes, she thought, she could do with some of his flattery right now.

And then the door opened and a stranger walked in. She almost made a grab for a kitchen knife, but stopped herself in time. She couldn't afford to lose a customer, and this one looked harmless enough. Looked, in fact, downright interesting. If not unbelievable; he was shaking and closing an umbrella.

Smartly dressed in a town suit, he was obviously not a local. His boyish face had a cheeky expression though there were too many lines for him to be as young as he looked. He removed his derby with a flourish. He had that devil-may-care appearance she had noticed in some gamblers and outlaws and other desperadoes.

She smiled a welcome. 'Looks like you need a hot meal. I've got beef on the stove with potatoes, with pie and coffee to follow.'

He smiled back. 'That sounds fine to

me. My name's Sinclair and I'm from England, via New York and Washington — amongst other places.'

Mary-Jane was fascinated by his accent. Just imagine, a real live dude appearing in Silver Gulch out of the rain. It reminded her of the fairy tales of her childhood, where the prince shed his disguise and married the wood-cutter's daughter. She almost blushed and banged a few pots around to break the spell.

When she served his meal, she sat opposite.

'I've read about England, but can't really believe all that stuff about lords and earls and suchlike.'

Sinclair paused in his meal and took a sip of water to clear his throat. 'Some of it's true — but I'd be wary of believing too much of what they print in newspapers and magazines.

'Sometimes though . . . it's true I'd be an earl if I weren't regarded as the black sheep of the family. So my brother's the earl and good luck to him. I'm enjoying life with a regular allowance to stay away, you know.'

'What's it like in England, the part where your family lives?'

He shrugged. 'Pretty dull. It's just a big house set among wooded hills. Servants to wait on us — a bit of hunting and fishing.'

He grinned, as if it were nothing, and that lent him a dashing air, she thought. She was thrilled; an aristocrat here, in her restaurant. Riley would have had a fit — he'd always spoken against the English, although she wasn't clear why.

'I'm Mary-Jane — the daughter of a farmer.'

'Farmers are useful, Mary-Jane. My family own farms, but someone else works them. They're parasites, never done a day's work in their life. I was never able to fit in — I liked to get out and about, meet people, have a bet on a horse race, enjoy a few drinks in town. I kept running up card debts till the old man refused to pay any more — '

'Then don't play against Farnsworth, at the Five Aces.'

'The old man told me to walk after a more serious scrape. 'Go west, young man', that sort of thing. I took him at his word, so here I am.'

She marvelled. Paid to stay away from home, never to have to work, no more washing up . . .

Sinclair laughed as he pushed back his empty plate. 'I'm not really the worthless and idle son the old man thought. I'm not stupid at all, really — at least, I don't think so. I've studied all sorts of different things on my travels.'

Mary-Jane daydreamed of herself as the consort of an aristocrat, an almost-earl, with a fancy accent and paid to travel. A home with servants. She got up and took the empty platter to the kitchen and served up pie and coffee.

The dream persisted. Of course, it couldn't happen that way . . . could it?

★ ★ ★

Alice didn't have her mind on the game and chucked her cards on the table.

'That's it, boys — I'm not in the mood tonight. Must be the rain getting me down.'

The poker players leaned back, surprised. It was warm and dry in the back room of the baker's shop; the smell of new bread mingled with tobacco smoke.

'That's not like you, Alice. Usually you win.'

'Yeah, well, I'm restless, can't seem to settle to anything — if you make a run for the saloon I don't doubt Farnsworth will give you a game.'

'And take our last cent.'

'Don't I . . . usually?'

'Yeah, but you're not a professional gambler. With Farnsworth it's a business; with you it's just a game. If we lose to you it's because you're a better player, and we don't mind that.'

Alice shrugged, not really interested. They were all loggers, Bishop's men, and she liked taking money off them. Bishop's money. They were rough men, except for the one named Rudge; he didn't appear as callous as the rest. She preferred playing against the cowhands, but they wouldn't be visiting town in this weather.

'Got things on my mind tonight,' she muttered.

She knew what it was. She was getting the itch again. No matter how much she despised men, it seemed her body couldn't do without one. Jerry had been worthless and useless, lazy, a sponger and a no-good; he'd proved that all right when he finally skipped out and left her stranded in this dump — but, at least, he'd been there when she needed some loving.

She knew her face wasn't her fortune and didn't have the choice Mary-Jane had; she could pick and choose. Alice liked Mary-Jane, but there were times when she could hit her. She had only to beckon and Cade would come running — but the rancher wasn't going to look at her. Not unless he were blind drunk.

She turned on the loggers in barely suppressed fury.

'Go on, get out! Get outa here now!'

# 11

Keyhoe was not a man to give up without a struggle, even when there seemed little hope. He had survived in tight corners before. He let himself go with the flow of water, half-swimming and keeping his chin above the surface, breathing deeply when he got the chance.

He'd lost Tuttle's lantern somewhere, but clung fast to the shotgun. He seemed to have been existing in total blackness all his life, even though he knew that wasn't true. He'd probably been underground a few hours only; it just felt longer.

He had no sense of direction; sometimes the gallery narrowed, almost squeezing him; sometimes the roof came so low he thought he was in a dead end — but that couldn't be as the water still carried him relentlessly forward. He could hear nothing above the gurgling sound of water.

He existed in a world of blackness, of cold and moving water and rock that removed layers of skin. It was the thought of Mary-Jane that kept him going.

After an age he felt his feet dragging on a rocky bottom. The level must be falling. Then he found he could stand, cold and shivering, and he paused a moment to take long breaths. Was that . . . ? Yes, after a seemingly endless nightmare a faint light appeared ahead.

His spirit lifted immediately; there was a way out. He forged ahead with renewed energy, the water down to his knees and still falling. The light at the end of the tunnel was a magnet drawing him.

He reached the opening and half-staggered, half-climbed through. He was in the gulch below town and the rain was easing off; he was among trees and stars gleamed palely between fast-moving clouds.

A soft voice said, 'I see you are all right. That is good.'

Keyhoe turned slowly to see the smiling face of Wu. He was soaked to the skin and holding a pick-handle. 'You opened this up, Wu?'

'It seemed a way to help.'

'Damn right — you saved my life.'

Wu nodded, apparently satisfied, and started to walk uphill.

Keyhoe followed, grateful for a guide; he had only the vaguest idea where he was. Eventually they reached a few buildings where a light showed and, as he was walking through the mud of Main Street, Keyhoe realized he was alone. The Chinese had slipped away in the darkness.

'Thanks, Wu,' he called softly.

He climbed onto the boardwalk, and continued along to Tuttle's. He had no idea of the time, yet there was a lamp burning in the store.

He knew there would be a stove burning, hot coffee and dry clothes, so he pushed open the door and went in.

Tuttle looked up, mug in hand, and said, 'Waal, guess that's not just rain — and it's not the time of year for a swim in the river, so . . . ?'

Keyhoe began to explain but Tuttle cut him short with a nod. 'Afterwards. Get out of those wet clothes first.' He reached for the shotgun and broke it open to dry out, removing one unused shell. 'Lost my lantern, have you?'

Keyhoe nodded and followed him into the back room, shedding his wet things. There seemed to be more stuff here than out front. Tuttle measured him with his eyes and sorted an outfit that more or less fitted. 'Have to do till your own dry.'

They sat by the stove, drinking hot strong coffee while Keyhoe told his story and Tuttle listened.

'Pulling away a pit prop in a mine — that's attempted murder. This ghost feller's stepping up the pressure, ain't he?'

'Figure to have a serious talk with

him next time we meet,' Keyhoe said mildly.

'Yeah, interesting it was Wu who got you out. Regular feller for keeping things to himself. I wonder what else he knows.' Tuttle poured more coffee. 'Let's see that ring you found.'

Keyhoe showed it, a plain gold band, and rubbed it clean. 'I counted seven bodies. That about right?'

'Exactly right, and this could be Riley's. I ain't no expert, but it's likely enough. Far as I remember, he was one of the few married men. Mary-Jane will know, but I suggest leaving it till morning — no sense upsetting her this time of night. She still relives that tragedy — maybe this will help.'

Keyhoe nodded agreement and slipped the ring back in his pocket.

'Had our own bit of excitement while you were after that ghost. The coach Anson left on brought a dude feller — sleeping at the hotel, so you've got company. English, he claims he's got business here. Comes from New York and Washington — '

'Washington?'

'Yeah.' Tuttle's sharp eyes regarded him closely. 'That mean something?'

'Could be.' Keyhoe suddenly recalled Anson telling him and Farnsworth that his client was not a local man, but came from Washington.

'Is this dude a lawyer?'

'He didn't say. Why?'

'Something Anson let slip.' Keyhoe shrugged. 'I'm off to bed.'

\* \* \*

In the morning, Keyhoe was awakened by a door banging and a strange voice swearing and he remembered the new arrival. Reluctantly, but curious, he rolled out of bed and dressed in the clothes borrowed from Tuttle.

Outside, the dude, half-dressed was at the yard pump. When he saw Keyhoe he demanded. 'Are we expected to wash outside in cold water? What kind of a hotel is this?'

'The kind that shut down — guess you must be the lawyer from Washington.'

The dude stared blankly at him. 'Lawyer? Where did you get that idea? My name's Sinclair and I'm from England — I passed through Washington on the way here, that's all. I've never worked in my life, as a lawyer or anything else, and don't intend to.'

He gestured at their surroundings. 'I am not used to this sort of place. I find this town depressingly crude.'

Keyhoe smiled. 'I suppose it is but, if you stay, you'll get used to it.'

'Oh, I'll stay.'

Keyhoe sluiced under the pump and turned back to his room. 'Coming for breakfast? Name's Keyhoe, and I'm the town dentist.'

'Breakfast, yes. The one bright spot in this god-forsaken hole — Mary-Jane.'

Someone had placed a couple of planks, end to end, across the mud of Main Street, and they made use of them.

As they paraded along the boardwalk, Keyhoe asked, 'Did you ever meet a feller named Anson?'

'Anson? I don't think so. I've heard the name somewhere, but I've never met him. Why?'

'Oh, it's just coincidence, I suppose, but he left town on the coach you arrived on.'

'It was raining hard at the time. Someone did pass me, going in the opposite direction, but I didn't take that much notice. Dash it all, I wasn't expecting to see anybody I knew in this back of beyond.'

It didn't seem that the dude was the mysterious buyer after all, but still Keyhoe wondered. The idea nagged at him that there had to be some connection with Sinclair's arrival.

When they got to the restaurant, they sat at the same table.

Mary-Jane said, 'Hi, Phil, business is looking up. I see you've met our English visitor . . . where did you get those clothes?'

Without waiting for an answer, she bustled off and returned with a platter of flapjacks and coffee. 'There's more of the same if you boys want it.'

They ate, Keyhoe ravenously after his underground adventure, Sinclair fastidiously. Afterwards, Keyhoe produced the wedding ring.

Mary-Jane's face lost colour. 'Where did you get this?'

'I followed the so-called ghost down the mine yesterday — and found seven bodies. If this is your husband's, I can confirm his death.'

Mary-Jane took the gold band and turned it slowly between her fingers. Tears came to her eyes.

'Yes,' she said quietly. 'This is the ring I gave to Riley, the ring my mother gave to my father. I'd know it anywhere.'

For a long moment, Keyhoe held her while she sobbed her relief from doubt. When they parted, Sinclair had gone, leaving a dollar on the table.

★  ★  ★

Sinclair felt amusement bubble to the surface. The town was a dump, yet it held a gem in Mary-Jane; of course she would have admirers — but a dentist? He had difficulty in taking Keyhoe seriously; he had never imagined a dentist courting.

So she was a widow. Well, he'd met widows before and found them satisfactory, always experienced, but without the drawback of a husband to show up at an inconvenient moment.

And what was all that nonsense about a ghost? Well, for the moment he would forget about Mary-Jane. There was something here he didn't understand.

His Washington contact hadn't indicated this business was *sub judice*, so it was a surprise that no-one in Silver Gulch appeared to know what was happening. That, of course, was why the town was so empty. The news hadn't spread yet, but when it did . . .

It was obvious that Keyhoe suspected something, but there was no hurry now. He had all the time in the world.

As he stood on the boardwalk, surveying the town, a lone rider came along the street. A cowboy, he assumed from the wide-brimmed hat and leggings; he had a bundle of fur tied behind the saddle and the horse kept shying. It smelt terrible.

Fascinated, Sinclair pointed to the bundle behind the saddle and called to the rider: 'What's the fur for?'

The cowboy reined back his horse and sat staring at him, a frown on his face. 'Ain't seen you before.' There was a hint of suspicion in his voice.

'Just arrived last night, from England.' Sinclair repeated his question.

'Bearskin for Mary-Jane. It's a gift.'

This one isn't quite all there, Sinclair thought. 'It's usual to cure a skin before presenting it to a lady. It stinks right now.'

'That right?' The cowboy looked doubtful, and sniffed the air. 'I can cure it, but that takes time.'

'Is there some hurry? And where can I get a horse?'

'Horse? Tuttle has a stable behind his store. He rents out.'

'Thanks.' Sinclair continued towards the general store, leaving the simple-minded cowboy sitting on his horse in Main Street with a puzzled expression.

# 12

Alice hitched up her gunbelt as she waited on the boardwalk. She'd caught a glimpse of the dude as he went into Tuttle's and was waiting for him to come out.

He finally appeared from the alley leading from the stable at the rear of the store, and she shouted, 'Hang on a minute, mister!'

He stopped, and she walked around him, inspecting him as if he were an exhibit at a freak show. She had to admit there was something eye-catching about him; the derby hat over blond hair, the expensive suiting, the blue eyes in a fresh complexion.

'Did you want to speak to me?' he asked politely, and his accent almost caused her to fall off the boardwalk.

'Guess it's you, right enough. I heard there was a dude in town and just wanted a look-see. Often heard of a dude out west but never seen one before. I'm Alice, and if you want bread or a seat in a poker school, you come to me.'

'Alice?' he said doubtfully, running an eye over her male outfit. 'Yes, I see now. You have the kind of homely face that could grow on me.'

'I've had worse said. Don't mean I'm not a woman underneath if you feel lonely one night.'

'I hardly think — '

'Oh, I know what you think. Like the rest, you fancy Mary-Jane, and I'll tell you right now you don't have a chance in hell. Now me, if you ask politely . . . waal, just maybe, if I'm in the mood.'

He didn't laugh, or look scared off. A knowing dude, this one, she thought. 'What were you up to in the stable?'

'Seeing about a horse — '

She smiled. 'Waal, don't let one of Cade's Texans hear you boast you can ride. They've got a special bronc for bucking off dudes.'

His gaze rested on her holstered revolver. 'And I can shoot straight too.'

'Yeah? Maybe you ain't just a tailor's dummy. Maybe we'll have a little sporting bet on that? That's if you're staying in Silver Gulch.'

'I'm staying — got a little business here.'

'Business, is it?' Suddenly, she was alert. 'Anything to do with town lots?'

His expression changed, the easy smile vanished. 'That's my business.'

''Cause if it is, I ain't selling, Mister — ?'

'Sinclair. About that sporting bet . . . how much are you willing to wager?'

★   ★   ★

Keyhoe was in Tuttle's general store, changing back into his own clothes, now dry, when Farnsworth looked in and said, cheerfully: 'If you want to see shooting or lay a bet, now's the time. It starts any minute.'

'Shooting?' Keyhoe was startled.

'Alice and the dude are shooting it out. Target shooting. I'm judge, so I'd better not take any bets myself.'

'I'll bet on Alice any day,' Tuttle said, and added to Keyhoe: 'We have to make our own entertainment here.'

Outside and further along the boardwalk, Farnsworth was tacking up four aces from a pack of cards to the wall of a derelict hut. Alice, scowling, loosened her revolver in its holster; Sinclair appeared completely relaxed, revolver held down at his side.

'The rules are simple,' Farnsworth said: 'Each shootist takes a turn. Alice has the heart and diamond; Mr Sinclair takes the club and spade. I count the hits — any doubtful hits and my judgement rules. Three shots at each card, alternately.'

He asked the contestants: 'Are you both ready?'

'Get on with it,' Alice said. Sinclair nodded.

'I've checked both weapons, Colt .44

revolvers. Lady first, if you will . . . may the best shootist win . . . fire at will.'

Keyhoe assumed Alice could shoot; it was the dude he was interested in. How a man performed in public could be a give-away . . . if he had something to hide.

Waiting, he decided he wasn't going down a mine ever again, not even for Mary-Jane. He'd keep watch on North End, but on the surface. If the ghost showed again, he'd just have to move faster and shoot quicker.

Alice half-crouched. Her hand blurred, bringing the gun from its holster and firing from the hip, one, two, three.

'One heart, two close,' Farnsworth chanted. 'Mr Sinclair, please.'

Keyhoe watched closely as the dude stepped up to the mark. Classic stance, two-handed grip; someone had trained him well. No attempt at speed; cool and deliberate, accuracy first. His aim was rock steady, each shot spaced out.

'Two clubs, one close. Alice on the diamond next.'

She took her second card more slowly.

'Two diamonds, one close. Good shooting Alice.'

Her smile was grim. 'I just think of the target as my opponent.'

Sinclair ignored the comment. It seemed nothing could disturb his careful aim. He sent three bullets at the ace of spades.

'Two spades, one close,' Farnsworth said. 'I declare Mr Sinclair the winner — pay all bets now.'

Alice flared up immediately. 'It was fixed . . . a put-up job. You bloody men always stick together, don't you?' She stalked off in a huff, reloading her revolver as she crossed the street. 'Damn dude!' she yelled back. 'Why don't you clear off to England?'

Farnsworth winked at Keyhoe.

★　★　★

Bishop was not in a good mood as he trudged through the mud to his house, a solid structure that looked more like a fort than a home. He had modelled it after a fort, and it had many rooms, most of them empty as yet; but he had plans. He lived apart from the men, except for Gregson, who had his uses.

He was tired, dirty and fed up. Sometimes it seemed to him he was the only man on the job with any savvy. The engine that drove the five-foot circular saw had broken down again; it was the fault of that idiot, Rudge, who didn't seem to have any mechanical sense whatsoever. But that didn't change the fact it was always himself who had to put things right. No one else was capable.

A bit different from his previous life; that had been one disaster after another. Whatever job he'd tried, at some point he lost his temper and smashed things up. The story of his life . . .

As a child he'd thrown tantrums as soon as he caught on he could get his own way by doing that. He'd learnt early in life he could always get what he wanted by threatening to torture the family dog. His parents had been weaklings; he saw that clearly now and despised them. In their place he'd have laughed and said, 'Go right ahead!'

At one time they'd brought home a brain doctor to see him; he'd attacked the man with a poker and that stopped his nonsense. Hugo Bishop did what he liked, when he liked, to whom he liked. But now he was somebody, he was the one who put things right. And he was proud of that.

Timber suited him because he'd finally found a job he could do better than anyone else. He'd made money and bought a half-share in the business. He'd been going up in the world until the silver ran out in Silver Gulch. He would have left except for Mary-Jane . . .

He reached his house of logs and

planks and climbed the steps to the big door, scraped the mud off his boots. The main room was still in darkness and, with a scowl, he jerked back the heavy curtain.

Gregson lay sprawled in a big chair, holding a bottle. He looked half-drunk.

Bishop, disgusted, snarled, 'Drinking at this time in the morning? Can't you leave the stuff alone for even five minutes?'

'You know I can't go into town for a drink because of that damned woman — '

Bishop walked forward to stand over him, hands clenched. 'If you go anywhere near Mary-Jane again, I'll feed you to the saw. And that's a promise.'

Gregson had taken enough liquor to answer back; he said, sullenly, 'You told me before. So what?'

Bishop looked around the room. 'I've also told you to clean this place.'

'Tomorrow, boss, tomorrow. Right now, I've got a helluva hangover.'

'You're forgetting your place, Gregson.'

'And you're forgetting I can talk. Maybe your partner having an accident with the saw wasn't so accidental?' Gregson smirked, pleased with himself. 'Sort of leaves you as sole owner, doesn't it?'

'Don't threaten me, Gregson.'

'Aw, lay off, boss. I'd be all right if I could get out. It's being stuck here — it's enough to drive a man right round the bend.'

'The rain's stopped. You could go hunting.'

'Yeah, that's right . . . hunting.' A light shone in Gregson's eyes as he thought about it. 'Yeah, Hugo, that's a real good idea. Hunting . . .'

# 13

Alice was baking bread, a job she usually enjoyed. She had her shirt sleeves rolled up, her arms covered in flour and the oven going. The smell of baking bread was an aroma that pleased her.

It was hot in her small shop and she had the door wide open to the street, her gun-belt hanging on a wall peg. She was not in a good mood today. It infuriated her that the dude had beaten her and she had lost her temper; she should have played it cool. She was furious with Mary-Jane, who seemed to be falling for that damned dentist when she had the chance of her own life. Waal, she could do something about Mary-Jane. She smiled grimly. The dude she needn't see — although it upset her that she felt she needed to avoid a man. She'd paid the money she'd lost on the bet to Farnsworth; keeping a straight face, he'd said he would see Mr Sinclair got it.

She decided to bake a pie and picked up a rolling pin. She had her back to the door so she had no warning. An arm went around her, dragging her backwards and a knife was held in front of her eyes.

A whispered voice: 'Not so bold without your gun, are you, Alice?'

She smelt whiskey and her pulse raced. Gregson!

'Run me outa town, will yuh, bitch! I'm goin' to carve my initials on your ugly mug so everyone will know who bested yuh — though maybe it'll improve your looks!'

He laughed, and Alice cursed. She kicked and threw the rolling pin backwards; it missed.

She fought with all her strength, twisting this way and that, trying to ignore the knife, the blood running down her face. She fought in silence, saving her breath, driven by a powerful hatred.

The knife hurt as it cut flesh, but he was too big, too heavy for her; he had muscles developed by chopping tall timber and it looked as though she were doomed to carry his brand.

A voice said, 'Is this — ?'

Gregson gave a startled cry and released her. She turned quickly, wiping blood from her eyes and groping for her gun. But that wasn't necessary.

The English dude was lashing Gregson with his cane as if he were beating a carpet.

'You nasty little thug,' he said. 'In my country, you would be whipped for attacking a woman.'

The cane descended again and again, bringing weals to the logger's face and arms as he tried to protect himself from Sinclair's furious onslaught. Even though he had another big Bowie knife in his hand, he cowered away from the cane.

'Go it, dude,' Alice said. 'Give him a few for me!'

Sinclair obeyed, vigorously, until Gregson, desperate, lowered his head and charged through the doorway, butting his slight form aside. He got in one last lash of the cane as Gregson, not stopping to retaliate, ran north up Main Street.

Sinclair got his breath back and let his grim expression relax in a smile. He offered her the rolling pin. 'I saw this come through the doorway.'

'Good thing for me you did,' Alice said solemnly. 'Dude, I owe you one.' She wiped blood and tears from her face and they stared at each other and then burst out laughing.

'I hope to do business with a man called Hugo Bishop. I imagine you can tell me where to find him.'

Alice stared at him.

'Yeah.' Alice pointed. 'Follow the trail up the gulch and you'll reach Bishop's place. You'll hear his sawmill going, and he's got a big house built like a fort.'

She paused. 'Let me advise yuh. Be right wary of any dealings with Hugo Bishop. I'd as soon trust a rattlesnake.'

He tipped his hat to her. 'Thanks for

the warning, Alice. But this is just a bit of business.'

'One more thing,' she said. 'Gregson works for Bishop.'

★ ★ ★

Sinclair rode a horse rented from Tuttle up the trail through the gulch. There was only one trail and the horse plodded through the mud between pines and firs. The rain had cleared but water still dripped from branches; it was not a bit like hunting in the shires back home.

He smiled as he thought of Alice, and frowned when he remembered Gregson. He'd have a word with Bishop about that one.

Presently he heard the screech of a saw going through timber, and saw the mill. The saw was steam-powered and there was a stack of logs beside it. A few wooden huts were dotted about and men were loading planks onto a wagon.

He rode up to them. 'Where can I

find Mr Bishop?'

One man paused in loading to jerk a thumb up the slope. Sinclair saw a large house built entirely of wood; it looked solid enough to be defended against an invading army. He rode to the front door, dismounted and hitched his horse before climbing the steps.

He rapped on the door and called out, 'Mr Bishop?'

After a while, the door opened and a man in a corduroy suit stood there, filling the doorway. 'I'm Bishop — who the hell are you and what d'you want?'

'My name is Sinclair and I'm from England. We have a mutual friend in Washington, a lawyer, and he told me what's about to happen here.'

'Did he, now?' Bishop scowled.

'It seemed to me an opportunity to make some money, so I came along to buy in.'

Bishop made no offer to invite him inside. He stared at him in disbelief. 'Buy in . . . ?'

'Yes. It's a business deal, isn't it? I

have some money to invest. Surely you won't turn down a partner with something to put in the kitty? I can offer — '

'Won't I?' Bishop laughed harshly. 'Limey, you've got it all wrong. Deals are for Washington — this is the frontier and we make our own chances. At gunpoint, if necessary. I don't need you, so get the hell off my land — and keep your mouth shut.'

Sinclair persisted. 'None of the town's people are in this with you?'

'Nobody's in it with me. Nobody! Silver Gulch is my town — mine!' Hugo Bishop was spluttering, his face purple and his hands clenched into fists. A wild look came to his eyes.

'Get off my land and out of my town . . . and don't tell those fools anything or it'll be the worse for you. I'll, I'll — ' Bishop appeared to be having trouble expressing himself fully.

Sinclair stared at the timber boss in amazement. 'Steady on, old chap, or you'll have a seizure.'

'Waal,' came a vicious voice from behind. 'If it ain't fancy pants.' A heavy fist rabbit-punched him and he fell face down on the steps.

For a moment, Sinclair thought he was paralysed; then the pain came. Reluctant to move, he watched two pairs of boots and listened to the voices.

'When I want someone beat up, I'll tell you. What was that all about?'

'I want this one to play with. See what he did to my face and arms?' Gregson's voice was the snarl of an animal. 'I'll feed him to the saw bit by bit. I'll cut out his guts and tie him up with them. I'll — '

'You won't. You'll do nothing that leaves a mark on him — this dude could be someone important . . . you can tell me why he picked on you.'

'I was just carving my initials on that woman — '

'Mary-Jane?' Bishop's voice rose sharply.

'No. The other one. Alice.'

'You're a fool, Gregson. I've told you

before, you can't take liberties with any woman out west. You ask for trouble. This dude might well have connections in Washington — and I don't want a US marshal sticking his nose into my affairs.'

'Hell!'

Through half-closed eyes, Sinclair saw the boot coming and rolled aside to miss the full force of the kick.

'Shamming, huh!'

'On second thoughts,' Bishop said, 'he knows something — it would be best to keep him out of circulation for a time. Tie him up and shut him away in one of the empty rooms.'

Sinclair almost made it to his knees when Gregson hit him again. The logger grabbed an ankle and dragged him into the house and across the floor, along a passage and into a bare room.

Bishop followed with a length of rope. 'Tie and gag him. Fix the door so it can't be opened from inside. Board over the window.'

Sinclair said nothing. There was

nothing to say with his hands tied. Gregson was smiling as he tied his ankles.

'I'm goin' to have fun with you, limey. It's just postponed, is all.'

The door closed and, presently, he heard hammering. The door was nailed shut. He heard hammering at the window and darkness came.

Sinclair lay on the floor in pain. It was cold. With a sigh, he reflected that he should have heeded Alice's warning.

\* \* \*

'Keep still,' Mary-Jane said, gently rubbing a salve into the cuts on Alice's face.

When Alice had arrived, Mary-Jane had been in the kitchen, humming as she worked. She knew what that meant; Mary-Jane had to be saved from herself.

'I'm going after Gregson,' she said, 'and I'm going to defenestrate him.' It was a word she'd read somewhere; she didn't know what it meant but it sounded unpleasant. 'All men should be defenestrated. Gregson's just one example.'

'I don't know,' Mary-Jane said. 'Since Phil found my ring down the mine, I've slept better. I'm sure now there's nothing to that ghost story and Riley died with the others in the disaster. I feel like a heavy weight has been lifted from my shoulders.'

Yeah, I know, Alice thought. She's got it bad for that damned dentist. Not that she had anything personal against Keyhoe, except he was a man.

'I heard about it. Maybe you can settle now, and forget about men altogether.'

Mary-Jane smiled. 'It's not quite like that. Phil — '

'You can't trust any of them. I know, Mary-Jane — you give one the cold shoulder and he comes running to me for consolation.' A little lie never hurt anyone, Alice thought. 'Earlier today I had to chase that dentist feller — he left a whole pack of toothpicks last night.'

'You mean . . . Phil?'

'Yeah, that one.' Mary-Jane had gone satisfyingly pale. 'Thanks for the treatment.'

As she went out through the doorway, hiding a smile, Mary-Jane sat down heavily. That was Keyhoe fixed. Oh, well, it was for her own good.

★ ★ ★

Alice's face was still painful as the sun went down and shadows gathered. She realized she wasn't going to get much sleep and decided a drink would help. She was not a hard-drinking woman, but still she enjoyed one now and again. Closing her shop, she crossed Main Street towards the Five Aces.

Tuttle stood on the boardwalk outside his store, looking anxiously both ways. He called, 'Seen the dude around, Alice?'

'Not lately. You lost him?'

'Lost my horse,' Tuttle said. 'The

dude rented him and I ain't seen him since.'

Alice paused. The dude on a horse; maybe that would be something to see.

'Figure he can ride well enough?'

'He can ride. Said he had some business to attend to.'

She remembered he'd said he was going to see Bishop. And Gregson was there. Would he stay overnight? Forget it. Something had happened to him. Gregson, of course. Shot? Lying on the cold ground somewhere?

Hell, he was old enough to look out for himself — but her face would be a lot worse if he hadn't stopped the lumberjack with the big knife.

'I'll go get him,' she said. 'I know where he is.'

'My horse,' Tuttle reminded her. 'Bring back my horse.'

She continued to the saloon and Farnsworth poured her a brandy without comment. 'On the house, Alice.'

'Thanks.' She drained the glass, hitched her gunbelt, and moved towards the batwings. It looked as if she wouldn't be getting any sleep tonight.

'Got to see a horse about a man.'

# 14

Alice walked between the trees to avoid the muddy trail as she went up the gulch. Cloud was thickening, reducing the amount of light, but she knew the way. She had visited the loggers' camp when the mine was still going and Bishop's partner had been alive. There had been rumours at the time, but nothing had ever been proved and now visitors were not welcome.

She was reluctant to admit she worried about the dude but, if he was in Gregson's hands, the sooner she got to him the better. She moved carefully to make as little noise as possible, ducking under low branches and avoiding dense undergrowth. There was no reason for Bishop to post a sentry, but that didn't mean he wouldn't. She aimed to approach undetected and snoop around to locate Sinclair; then she'd decide what to do.

A light glimmered between the trees, and she slowed down. The saw was quiet so work had shut down; a few lights came from scattered cabins. She drew her revolver as she sneaked closer to the big house where Bishop lived; big and solid, it looked like a fortress against the night sky. Many of its windows remained in darkness, but a lamp glowed in the main room. Bishop or Gregson, or both, were still up and about.

She backed off and circled to investigate some outbuildings. There were sounds of movement from one, even though it was unlighted; she paused, listening, and investigated cautiously.

The building was a stable for the heavy horses that drew the lumber wagon. There was another horse, saddled: Tuttle's, and that proved Sinclair was still here. But alive, or dead?

She went around the big house again till she found a window boarded up. Why? She edged closer, all senses alert, and peered through a crack between the timbers. It was dark inside, but she could hear someone moving and she called softly, 'Dude?'

The sounds stopped. A silence dragged. Then came a slithering sound across bare boards and a tapping at the wall below the window.

He was there, still alive, but hurt? Tied up? He couldn't speak, but she heard sounds of a struggle. All she had to do now was get him out and away.

★　★　★

Sinclair was not a happy man. He was not used to being treated like an object. The back of his neck hurt and his ribs ached. Bits of skin were missing where he'd been dragged across rough planking; and he was cold.

He didn't mind missing a meal, but

to have no water and a filthy gag in his mouth nearly choking him was severe punishment.

His legs and arms were numb where the ropes bit into his flesh; Gregson had drawn them cruelly tight. Even if he could somehow get free, it would be a long time before he would be able to walk.

He concentrated on trying to fray one of the ropes against a nail that projected from a piece of planking. It was a hopeless task but kept his mind occupied. He really should have taken more notice of what Alice said. Not only was Gregson a brute, but it appeared that Bishop was a madman.

He heard a faint sound at the window. Was there really someone there? Then came a whisper, 'Dude?'

He didn't recognize the voice, but hope blossomed. He wriggled across the floorboards towards the window, cursing the gag that prevented him answering. He reached the plank wall and tapped it with a boot to let whoever know was out there he was a prisoner.

What now? he wondered.

★ ★ ★

Alice whispered encouragement. 'I'm getting you out, dude. Just hang on.'

She moved quietly along the side of the house and around the corner to the lighted window of the main room. She wanted to know if Bishop was likely to stroll around, or hit his bed.

'You going to sit there drinking all night, Gregson?'

'I'll stop quick enough if you let me at the English dude.'

'You'll leave him alone. I've got some thinking to do — it's possible they'll miss him in town.'

'So what?'

'Sober up, and get some sleep. I may need you for something tomorrow.'

Alice drifted silently away to a patch of deep shadow and waited, watching and listening. The lights in the loggers' huts went out one by one. She began to freeze as the temperature dropped.

It looked as though the dude might not be able to hurry if he'd been seriously hurt; and there was little chance of opening a nailed-up window without some noise. She needed a tool of some sort, and a distraction to keep attention away from her.

She returned to the stable and searched around and found a metal crow-bar to lever the boards away. This was a timber camp, she thought; fire was a natural enemy. With a fire starting, everyone would be busy putting it out.

The sawmill: they'd give priority to saving the big saw, that was certain sure. And there'd be sawdust and off-cuts and discards.

She went quietly down the hillside in the shadows. She neither saw nor heard anyone.

The shed with the big circular saw was dark and still. She made a short trail of wood dust and small chips to another, bigger pile. There were short pieces of timber stacked to one side.

Alice always carried matches for her oven and lamp. She struck one, shielding the flame with her body. The wood was still damp, and she got smoke but no flame; she cursed softly and struck another match. This time there was a spark and then a small flame. The trail she had laid began to burn, and she turned away and ran uphill. Speed counted now.

She went first to the stable and brought out Tuttle's horse; Sinclair might need that. She led it into the trees and tied it with a quick-release knot. At the boarded window, she whispered, 'Soon, dude.'

He tapped back.

She waited. A tiny red glow began to blossom, then came a raised voice, 'Fire!' Men, cursing, half-dressed ran towards the sawmill shed.

Alice added her voice to the noise: 'Fire! Fire!'

Bishop turned out, pushing Gregson in front of him. 'Water! Get buckets!'

'Any minute now, dude.'

Alice didn't wait any longer; she used the metal crow-bar to lever the boards away from the window frame. The screech of nails withdrawing set her teeth on edge, but no one seemed to notice.

She got the boards off and peered in; a dark form lay on the floor below the window. She climbed through and removed his gag, and then realized he was tied securely and she hadn't planned as well as she thought.

'Damn — forgot a knife.'

She hoisted him upright and pushed him out through the window; a few more bruises wouldn't kill him. Outside, she dragged him into deep shadow.

'I'll get a knife,' she hissed, and moved quietly towards the stable.

She stopped; someone was running towards her. She dropped flat and waited; the running man passed her and went towards the stable. Another oversight; it was the driver going to get his horses out.

Alice came upright and followed quickly. She let him open the door and get inside, then she slugged him with the barrel of her revolver.

At least she didn't have to search for a knife now; the driver had one sheathed at his waist. She returned to Sinclair and cut him free.

The dude croaked, 'Can't walk — tied too tight.'

'Stop worrying — I've got your horse waiting.'

She hauled him upright, and put an arm around him, half-carrying, half-dragging him to where she'd left Tuttle's horse. She helped him into the saddle and led the horse downhill between the trees.

She left behind a smell of smoke and the sound of men cursing. 'That'll give them something else to worry about besides us.'

She paused further down the track where the leaves of shrubs still held some rain water and gave Sinclair a taste of wetness to ease his throat.

He smiled for her, and croaked, 'Alice, I owe you one.'

* * *

Bishop raved like a madman until the fire was under control. 'I've told you men, again and again — don't smoke on the job. Some double-damned fool dropped a lighted cigarette, and when I find out who it is — '

Gregson saw the men were irritated. It was early morning and it was cold, they'd lost sleep and put out a fire; but instead of praise and thanks, they got bawled out.

'Lucky the wood was still damp,' he said. 'No great harm done, boss.'

Bishop glared at him. 'The horses. What happened with them?'

Gregson realized he hadn't seen the driver, and took the chance to go up the hill out of Bishop's way. He met the driver coming down.

'What happened to you?'

'Someone slugged me. I've only just

come round — the horses are okay, but the saddled one has gone.'

'What!'

Gregson broke into a run, heading for the big house. He went around the side to the window he had boarded over and saw the planks on the ground. He stuck his head inside, and then shouted down the hillside: 'Hugo, the dude's gone!'

When Bishop hurried up, Gregson said, 'Someone's got him out, and his horse too — they're likely back in town by now. That someone started the fire to get us out of the house.'

'Damn, damn, damn!' Bishop raved like a maniac. 'By now the whole town knows — that dude will spread the word. I'll ride in with every man armed. I'll kill those who won't sell . . . I'll fire the town . . . I'll burn them out. All of them. I want that town and Mary-Jane and, by god, I'll have them. No one can stop me — '

Gregson tried to quieten him.

'Not now, boss. The men are fed up.

Let them sleep and have a meal first. Then, perhaps . . . '

★　★　★

Sinclair was beginning to revive as he rode down the trail to North End, his horse still led by Alice. He had made a serious mistake, and was badly shaken; he'd never come across anyone like Hugo Bishop before. Alice too, he thought, had underestimated the timber boss.

She let the horse find its own footing through the mud and eventually they arrived on Main Street — though not before he'd looked over his shoulder a few times to make sure they weren't being followed.

He said, 'This'll do,' when they reached the Five Aces. 'I need a drink.'

Alice hitched the horse, and Sinclair slid from the saddle. Tuttle was talking to the saloon-keeper and both stared when Alice helped the dude through the batwings.

'Looks like you had a fight, friend. I've heard about you — my name's Farnsworth. Get that down you.'

He poured a brandy and Sinclair gulped it in one swallow and held out his glass for a refill. Farnsworth poured again, and Sinclair sat in a chair and sipped the brandy this time.

'I really needed that . . . good stuff this. Give my friend Alice one — I'm paying.'

'From my private stock.'

'Many thanks.' Sinclair raised his glass in a toast. 'I want everybody to join me in thanking Alice for rescuing me from that madman.'

'Is my horse all right?' Tuttle asked.

'Better than the dude,' Alice said. 'And hitched outside.'

'So what happened? Did you see our Hugo?'

Sinclair made a face. 'Yes, I saw him, and I don't care if I never see him again. The man's a lunatic, practically frothing at the mouth. Apparently, it's supposed to be a secret he's buying up town lots — I wanted to deal myself in, that's all. Just put up some money, in the normal way of business — and he went berserk. He's stark raving mad.'

Tuttle looked at Farnsworth, who nodded. 'So it's Bishop — d'yuh know why?'

'Of course: a railroad is coming through here on the way west.'

'I guessed it had to be something like that,' Tuttle said. 'A railroad, yes . . . that could mean a lot of people travelling, a lot of business. I propose to call a town meeting in the morning — say, ten o'clock, to discuss this. Will you be prepared to repeat your story, Mr Sinclair?'

'Why not? It's true — and I'll tell you something else, that man's dangerous. He's not going to take his exposure quietly.'

# 15

Keyhoe sat alone at a table, a little apart from the others in the saloon. Farnsworth had donated a bottle of whiskey which was being passed around; Mary-Jane had brought a platter of her home-made biscuits.

Sinclair sat up front with Tuttle. The mayor didn't look too happy with the turn-out, but then there weren't that many folk left to turn out.

Mary-Jane sat with Alice, who seemed to be watching Sinclair and smiling to herself.

Keyhoe was puzzled. Since he'd found the ring Mary-Jane had given her husband, she seemed to have cooled off. She remained polite, but distant, and he couldn't figure out why. She seemed, if anything, to favour Sinclair now.

Was she just reacting to some

imagined slight? If so, what? He wasn't aware of having done anything to upset her. It was a mystery, but at the moment there were more important things to discuss. As soon as the present situation was dealt with, he'd need to talk seriously with Mary-Jane.

Tuttle rapped on the table with a glass. 'As mayor of Silver Gulch I've called this meeting because our visitor from England brings important news. You need to be aware of what's going on, and we have to decide, collectively, what to do about it.'

He paused to look at Sinclair, who shrugged.

Tuttle continued: 'Mr Sinclair tells me that he learnt from a contact in Washington that a railroad is to be built that passes through Silver Gulch to all points west.'

His listeners sat up and began to take a real interest.

'We know what that could mean: new life for this town, so that the lots we bought are worth real money again. We could even have another boomtime. At the very least, folk will be travelling this way in increasing numbers and that means extra business for all of us.

'The feller who tipped him off also told Hugo Bishop. Bishop is the mystery man behind Anson — getting lots cheap means he can sell at a profit when the town grows. It seems obvious now that he's likely the one behind the ghost scare too.'

Mary-Jane murmured, 'So it was Bishop after all frightening women and families out of town.'

Tuttle waited for silence. 'It appears, from what Mr Sinclair tells me, that Bishop intends to grab the rest of the town — by force, if necessary. We have to decide what we're going to do.'

Someone objected, 'Why should we believe this dude? He's a stranger.'

Alice scowled. 'I believe him — why else would Bishop want to keep him quiet?'

Sinclair said, with feeling: 'You didn't see and hear him. I did, and he scared me. He's insane, and seems to believe that a gun is the only law.'

'Bishop may be right about that,' Farnsworth added, 'and his loggers outnumber us.'

Mary-Jane looked troubled. 'Do we have to turn this into a fight? Can't the law handle it? Surely it can't be legal to scare people away so he can buy cheap?'

Alice laughed. 'You're an optimist, Mary-Jane.'

Keyhoe said, 'Even if the law were here, you'd need solid evidence to stand up in court.'

Farnsworth gave him a hard look. 'You know something about the law?'

'Only as a working cop back in the city. I do know, from experience, you'd need to get cast-iron proof to beat Bishop's lawyers.'

'So maybe we'll handle it out of court,' Alice said. 'Leaving town to find work is one thing — being forced out is another.'

Tuttle frowned. 'Some of us saw what

lawlessness could do during the early days of the silver strike. That's why we got together and appointed a town marshal. We don't want those days back. I say we appoint a new marshal to maintain order here, and I propose Phil Keyhoe — that is, if he's willing to stand.'

Keyhoe was unhappy about the prospect. Taking on Bishop's outfit would be no picnic — and he could still feel the beating the New York Hammers had inflicted.

Sinclair saw his hesitation, and added, 'It's not just the town he wants — it's Mary-Jane too.'

Tuttle sipped at his drink. 'If Phil agrees to take the job, it'll be up to the rest of us to support him. If he warns Bishop off, and Bishop ignores the warning, he places himself outside the law. In that case we stand behind our marshal.'

'We, at this meeting, constitute the town council and it's for us to decide. Can I have a vote for Keyhoe as town marshal? All in favour . . . '

Tuttle looked over the raised hands. 'Carried. Phil, will you accept the job?'

Keyhoe nodded; Bishop had to be stopped if Mary-Jane was threatened.

The mayor brought a metal badge from his pocket, polished it on his cuff and pinned it to Keyhoe's shirt. 'Now, Marshal, tell us what we must do.'

Keyhoe looked over the small gathering, and saw the Chinese man keeping his head down at the back.

'Wu, what can you tell us about Bishop's knowledge of the mine workings?'

'Gregson was a miner before he became a logger. Bishop gave him a job because he knew the old mine.'

'So it's near enough certain Gregson was playing the ghost at Bishop's order — I shall have to see Bishop and warn him off. We've got Mr Sinclair's assessment, but I need to make my own . . . and Alice's,' he added hastily as she glared at him.

He paused, looking them over. They

seemed determined enough, but they were few in numbers if it came to a fight.

'Remember, Bishop's men are a tough bunch and could likely run us off without much sweat. I suggest we warn the homesteaders and Mr Cade — both have an interest in who runs this town when the railroad comes through.'

He glanced at the dude. 'Mr Sinclair, are you with us? Even one extra may swing the tide against Bishop.'

'I shan't run from a bully. He treated me badly and threatened a lady.'

'Mary-Jane — '

She had her temper up. 'I'm staying right here and I'll be open for business as usual. Anyone who thinks he can run me out of town will get a surprise!'

'Meeting adjourned,' Tuttle said quickly. 'Marshal, come with me and I'll fit you out.'

Keyhoe walked with the mayor to his store, where he collected the shotgun; it had been cleaned, oiled and loaded. He thrust a handful of extra shells into his coat pocket. They went back to the stable behind the store.

'Are you a horseman?'

'I've never been on a horse in my life.'

'Then I'll give you Tildy, she's quiet enough.'

Though apprehensive, Keyhoe was intrigued. 'Isn't that an unusual name for a horse?'

'Horses get all kinds of names. This one was bought by a miner from Australia when silver was plentiful. She was young and lively and led him a right dance, so he called her 'Waltzing Matilda'! That got shortened to Tildy. Don't worry, she's a sedate old lady these days.'

Tuttle brought some lumps of sugar from his pocket and handed them to Keyhoe. 'Feed her one of these now and again and you'll have no trouble.'

He saddled the mare, tightened the girth and hoisted Keyhoe into the saddle. He looked at him sitting there, tall and straight, resting the shotgun across the saddle horn, and nodded.

'One more thing,' he said, and went back into his store; he returned with a cowpuncher's broad-brimmed hat. 'Try that for size. That's better. Man on a horse can look scary to a man on foot.

'Just relax and sit easy, the horse does the work. Leave Tildy alone and she'll take you where you want to get. She knows the trails — you just point her in the direction you want. A gentle pull on one rein will turn her. Uphill she's slow, so don't try to hurry her.'

Tuttle paused. 'And if you've got to use that gun, don't shoot from the saddle — dismount first.'

He led the horse out of the stable and down the side alley to Main Street. Alice waited on the boardwalk, and looked him over critically.

'Guess you'll have to do — Marshal. Just remember to shoot first.'

Tuttle pointed the mare at the slope and slapped her rump. Tildy plodded away, carrying the new marshal of Silver Gulch.

Keyhoe rode slowly through North End to where the gulch climbed towards the mountains. Tildy didn't like the mud, but kept moving forward at her own pace. Gradually the sun was hidden behind rock walls and tall trees and the air grew colder. Shadows closed in.

After a while he got used to Tildy's motion and decided riding wasn't all that bad. He began to relax. It was even pleasant jogging along with the shotgun resting lightly across the saddle horn; he had no intention of using it unless someone shot at him first. His idea was to cool down the hotheads and persuade Bishop to see reason. The last thing he wanted was to stir up trouble.

He saw the stumps of trees that had been felled and smelt fresh-cut timber. Then he came to a clearing where log huts had been built at random. The sawmill was not working.

In front of a big house, Hugo Bishop was talking to a group of loggers. As Keyhoe rode closer, he heard the timber boss arguing with one of his men.

'Don't try to tell me, Rudge. I'm telling you.'

Rudge said, 'We signed on to cut timber, that's all I'm saying.'

'You'll do whatever — '

Bishop paused as he noticed Keyhoe on Tildy. He didn't miss the shotgun, or the badge glinting in the sun.

He said, 'I own this property, dentist. If you're not off my land in thirty seconds, I'll run you off.'

Keyhoe kept his tone mild. 'Mr Sinclair has reported that you're trying to stir up trouble for the townsfolk. I've been appointed town marshal, and I won't have it. If you step outside the law, Mr Bishop, I'll show you the inside of our jail.'

Then he ignored the timber boss and turned to face the crowd of loggers.

'You men are still welcome in town when you're off duty, if you behave. I suggest you come a few at a time. But like your boss, go outside the law and you're going to land in trouble.'

There was hardly a murmur, and he realized Tuttle was right. People looked up to a man on a horse. He recalled a time in New York when he'd seen mounted police disperse a mob.

His attention moved back to Bishop, and caught a sly look on his face. Suddenly he understood he could never trust this man, no matter what he said.

'Surely you don't believe that fairy story the English dude dreamed up?'

Keyhoe shrugged. 'What I believe isn't important. It's the way you behave in town that's important — and that means you don't carry guns.'

He caught Bishop exchanging a glance with Gregson, standing at the back of the crowd. The logger appeared startled, and Keyhoe knew he hadn't heard of his escape from the mine.

'What I've said doesn't apply to you, Gregson. If you take one step across the town boundary, I'll slam you in jail immediately.'

He addressed the loggers again. 'The

whole town knows now that it was Gregson playing the ghost to scare women with families away. Is that the sort of rat you want to work with? Think about it.'

Keyhoe pulled lightly on one rein, and Tildy swung around and started back downhill. He sweated for a moment, waiting for a bullet in the back, but none came.

In the silence, he heard a sneer from Gregson, 'Who does he think he is?'

Bishop's voice came: 'I own that shack you're using, dentist — you owe me rent money, hear? And I'll be coming to collect.'

# 16

Once he got down below the evergreens and the sun warmed him through, Keyhoe was able to relax. Tildy plodded through the mud at her steady pace and eventually reached North End. The only activity was further along Main Street and he saw it was at the previous marshal's office. It seemed Tuttle was serious about upholding the law.

Mary-Jane glanced at him and looked away. 'Just giving your new office a clean out, Marshal.'

He noticed that Sinclair was close beside her — a bit too close — and smiling. 'And I'm fixing the jail so it'll hold that man Bishop. And Gregson.'

They seemed, Keyhoe thought sourly, to be working well together, and having a good time. The dude was handsome, he had to admit; expensively dressed, his blond hair brushed and shining. His expression was that bit cheeky; and why shouldn't it be? He had money and a title and Mary-Jane appeared to be enjoying his company.

Suddenly Keyhoe realized he was jealous . . . that's daft, he told himself. Mary-Jane wasn't the kind to be swayed by wealth — was she? He felt an edge of doubt. Was that why she seemed to have gone off him? Perhaps she was serious about Sinclair?

Tuttle finished nailing up a new sign.

'I sent Wu down to warn Nickson, who'll pass on the message to other homesteaders. Wu won't go near the Bar C, and I doubt if Nickson will either. There's no love lost there.'

'It's a start,' Keyhoe said. 'The news will soon get around.' But would it get around quickly enough to save them?

'How was Bishop?'

'Trying to talk his men into attacking us. I read them the rules, and it may hold them for a spell. But I don't trust Bishop, or Gregson. I suspect they'll persuade the loggers to move against us before long. We'd better let Cade know our position before that happens.'

Keyhoe noticed that Tildy was covered in sweat, and gave her a handful of sugar lumps. He turned her towards the stable to wipe her down.

★ ★ ★

Gregson liked being second-in-command to Bishop; it gave him power without responsibility. Let the boss do the worrying.

Even when young he'd had no desire to be the bully-in-chief; easier to follow a natural leader and pick on whoever was smaller and weaker. It had grown to be a way of life.

When he'd gone panning for gold he quickly learnt he didn't need to work; it was easier to let others do the panning and shoot them in the back. No one could identify gold dust.

When he'd been tempted down a mine by the promise of high wages, he'd soon found it easier to run errands for the boss and spy for him. Easier, and better paid.

Now it was Bishop . . . but he had a sneaking feeling he might be moving on shortly.

He scowled when he thought of Keyhoe, but he wasn't going to tackle him face to face. Keyhoe was too big for that. And the dude . . . he still had to get even there. Bishop was the key. Get him stirred up and, yes, he'd soon have the dentist and Sinclair and Alice and that stuck-up bitch Mary-Jane grovelling at his feet.

Gregson went up the steps and into the main room of the house and eyed his boss with sly amusement. This time he was the sober one while Bishop hit the bottle. He guessed that the dentist's visit had dented his boss's ego; he wasn't used to anyone talking back.

Gregson said easily, 'Forget about Keyhoe — '

'You told me he was dead!'

'I thought so. I still don't understand how he got out of the old mine, but somehow he must have done. He was real lucky.'

Gregson relaxed in a big chair, watching Bishop pace up and down. There were moments when he felt superior, and they were moments he savoured. He leaned forward to help himself to a cigar from the box on the table.

He struck a match and lit up. 'Forget the law bit. I figure Keyhoe's running a bluff. What can one man do? He's got no back-up. The sheriff is miles away and doesn't care what happens here.'

He puffed contentedly. Bishop didn't often smoke, but he insisted on the best.

'A few townsmen giving him a tin star doesn't make him immortal. Just one bullet will cut him down, and we've got the advantage of numbers.'

'Rudge is against —'

'Rudge talks too much. Boss, all you've got to do is offer the men a bonus and they'll do anything. Hell, there's almost no opposition in town.

Anyway, it's the woman Keyhoe is after — '

'Mary-Jane?' Bishop roused out of his drinking bout. 'If I thought Keyhoe — '

Gregson kept a smile off his face. He'd calculated that would stir him up. 'You can be damned sure he's after her. Seen 'em together, ain't I?'

'I'll kill him,' Bishop snarled. 'I'll gut-shoot him and watch him die slowly. I'll smash his kneecaps and watch him crawl. I'll — '

Gregson drew on his cigar. 'I've got a real neat idea to take Keyhoe out of our way. Leave that to me. You concentrate on getting the men into action.'

'You're right. Kill Keyhoe first — a law badge means nothing out here and, if Rudge objects, I'll sack him and run him off.'

Cunning showed in Bishop's eyes. 'Gregson, you kill the dentist for me and I'll pay yuh a bonus, say a hundred bucks, okay?'

'One hundred? For a lawman? Make

it five hundred and he won't touch Mary-Jane again.'

'Five hundred? Too much. Make it two fifty — now kill that son-of-a-bitch.'

Gregson crushed out his cigar. 'Okay. For what I have in mind, I'll need to borrow a horse.'

'Take mine.'

'Keyhoe was dead lucky last time . . . this time he'll just be dead.'

★   ★   ★

Silver Gulch was quiet. Keyhoe sat on a chair in the open doorway of the marshal's office, enjoying the last of the sun and watching the evening shadows gather on Main Street. The mud was slowly drying.

He brooded. Sinclair was apparently still in Mary-Jane's favour — and he needed a plan to combat the expected attack. Somehow they had to gain an element of surprise. His gaze lingered on the ruin of a bank further along the street. It was one of the few two-storey buildings, but decaying fast.

It was the outside staircase, leading up to where a door had been, that put the idea into his head. He sat up straight and studied the false fronts of the buildings. Most had them on both sides of Main Street. It might work — Tuttle was the man who'd know what was possible.

He left his seat and strode along the boardwalk to the store and found Tuttle cleaning his stock of guns and laying out ammunition on the counter. At first, the mayor scratched his head over Keyhoe's proposal but, gradually, he warmed to it.

'Yes, I see what you mean. If we take care setting it up, it should come as a complete surprise, and that will give us an initial advantage. Let's do it.'

From outside came a sound of hoofbeats. Despite the residue of mud, a rider was flogging his horse to its best speed. Frowning, Keyhoe snatched up his shotgun and stood in the doorway.

The rider, obscured by deepening shadow, was impossible to identify — but who else but a logger could be coming from North End?

The rider did not glance his way, but kept his head down as he continued past, and Keyhoe stared after him, wondering. Then, as the horseman reached his new office, a bundle arced through the air with sparks trailing. He rode on, disappearing among trees further down the gulch.

There was the sound of an explosion and Keyhoe and Tuttle ducked for cover.

Red and yellow flame blossomed. Clouds of smoke bellowed. Debris rained down. The marshal's new office had been ripped apart.

'Jeez!' Tuttle exclaimed. 'That was blasting powder — miners used the stuff, and I recognized Bishop's horse.'

Alice appeared from her shop. 'That was Gregson.'

A woman's scream erupted. Mary-Jane was running towards the fire.

Keyhoe stepped onto the plankwalk and shouted, 'I'm here, Mary-Jane.'

She stopped, and turned. Then she ran into his arms and clung to him. 'I thought . . . oh, Phil!'

Alice stared at the pair in disgust. 'The loving bit can wait — we've got a fire to deal with.'

'Buckets here,' Tuttle called. 'Make a chain from the pump.'

It was hard work for a time, but the fire was doused. The marshal's office and jail had vanished, but the town was saved. The heavy rain earlier had waterlogged most buildings; if it hadn't been for that, Silver Gulch could have been wiped out.

Sinclair looked at the still-smouldering ruin. 'They really meant to get you, Marshal. If you'd been inside, you wouldn't have stood a chance.'

'Bishop must be mad,' Mary-Jane said, her face still white.

'That's what I said before,' Sinclair pointed out. Farnsworth stared at the wreckage. 'All that work wasted.'

Tuttle smiled grimly. 'Before the town had a jail, we used shackles, chained 'em to the nearest tree. I've still got those shackles.'

Keyhoe smiled. 'So any troublemakers are due an extra surprise when they hit town.'

* * *

Gregson had the feeling Hugo Bishop had been eating loco weed. His boss was over the top with excitement and waving a handgun about in a way that alarmed him. He stepped back a pace.

He was feeling better now he'd destroyed Keyhoe and had an extra 250 dollars in his pocket. If things went wrong, he would duck out and vanish, leaving Bishop to go it alone.

The morning sun was warm and Gregson edged away from the crowd to take advantage of it. He was willing to do Bishop's dirty work for a price, but he didn't intend to be pulled down with him if anything went wrong. Of course, nothing could, but . . .

Bishop was behaving like a maniac, and Gregson liked to play it safe and look after number one. He'd done well out of playing the ghost and had a thick roll of notes and a tin box filled with coins safely hidden away.

'This will be easy,' Bishop told the loggers gathered around him. His voice had the ring of confidence. 'We'll ride into town on the wagon and just take it over. I've got forms from the lawyer — the few people left will sign if we put a bit of pressure on them. If they won't, we'll shoot them and throw the bodies down an old mine shaft. No one will ever find them, or care for that matter. If necessary, we'll burn the town to the ground. It's the land I want, not a few wood shacks.'

Rudge said, 'I don't like the sound of this, Mr Bishop.'

'You don't, Rudge? That's too bad, because I'm fed up with your whining. You're sacked — now get off my property immediately.'

'The rest of you — each man will get a bonus of one hundred dollars, paid in cash the moment the town is mine.' He paused, eyes glittering. 'On second thoughts, perhaps it would be best to start from the ground up . . . we'll build real houses, not shacks, and I'll rename the place Bishopstown!'

Gregson stifled his laughter. Yeah, pure loco. He noticed Rudge walking away; the hell with him, let him go. Even if he warned the townsmen, what could they do? Nothing.

He saw Bishop looking directly at him, and said hastily, 'Fine with me, boss. For an extra hundred bucks I'll enjoy making that stuck-up woman sign your bit of paper.'

Bishop glared. 'I've told you before, Gregson, you'll leave Mary-Jane to me.'

'Sure, boss,' he agreed hastily. But he thought, not if I catch her first.

'Right then.' Bishop was smiling, certain of success. 'Arm every man, Gregson. Get the big wagon and horses. There'll be little opposition. The dude is nothing — only Farnsworth might be tempted to make a fight of it, and I reckon he'll sign quick enough once he sees we mean business ... okay, let's go!'

*  *  *

Keyhoe was taking a drink with Farnsworth in the Five Aces. The saloon-keeper had brought the Sharps rifle from beneath the counter.

'Unfortunately, Tuttle doesn't have ammunition to fit, so I've only the few shells the Marchmonts carried. But I've put Bishop's name on one of them.'

Mary-Jane pushed through the batwings and announced, 'Man coming from North End. He looks harmless, but who knows?'

Keyhoe set down his glass and wiped the back of his hand across his mouth. He picked up the shotgun and went out onto the boardwalk. Farnsworth joined him.

One man, obviously a lumberjack, sat

astride a mule plodding towards them. Keyhoe recognized Rudge, the one man who had challenged Bishop.

It looked as if he might continue to ride south without pause, so Mary-Jane called, 'What's happening?'

Rudge reined in the mule and tipped his hat.

'I'm getting out while I can, ma'am. That Bishop's clean out of his mind — arming the men and promising a bonus when he grabs the town. He aims to force yuh to sign — or kill yuh all and burn the place down. Crazy man!'

'Thanks for the warning,' Keyhoe said.

'Yeah, well, they're getting the wagon now, the whole crew, twenty or more will be coming down. I don't want any part of it.'

Mary-Jane said, 'Help yourself to any food you want from my place. Take it with you.'

'Thanks, ma'am, I'll do that. Bishop and Gregson are leading them, and I sure don't aim to be here when that pair arrive. They're not far behind.'

Alice said, 'Or you could stay and fight with us.'

Rudge didn't bother to answer; he just set his mule in motion.

Keyhoe said, 'Mary-Jane, I want you to ride directly to Mr Cade and ask for help. He knows you and will take your word.'

He looked at Farnsworth. 'Time for us to get organized.'

This time, Mary-Jane didn't argue but hurried to the stable behind Tuttle's store and saddled the cow pony Cade had left there for her use. She took it slowly going downhill through drying mud, heading south towards the open range.

She passed Rudge on his mule and kept going; when she reached bare rock on the trail she used her heels to kick the pony up to speed. The animal responded immediately. Glad to be out again, she thought; she hadn't had much exercise lately. When Riley was alive ... she bit her lip; no sense following that thought. Now she had to save the new man in her life.

At the bottom of the hill she turned left onto grass and would have passed Nickson's homestead, but he was working among his crops and straightened up when he saw her.

She slowed briefly, thinking Bishop might not plan to leave witnesses alive if he carried through his threat, and shouted: 'Warn everybody — Bishop's threatened to kill all who won't sell. He's going to burn the town to the ground!'

She rode on, saving her horse because the cowhands might be scattered over the range. She glimpsed cattle near the river and headed that way; bound to find someone there. As she approached, a rider came from behind the herd to intercept her, and she recognized Logan, foreman of the Bar C.

'Hi, ma'am. You've just missed Mr Cade — he's gone back to the ranch.'

Tersely, she explained the situation. 'Can you help? How many men can you spare?'

Logan looked doubtful. 'Waal, now, guess I'll have to ask the boss.'

'There's no time to waste. Your boss will need the railroad to ship cattle east ... and we know now it was Gregson playing ghost. Obviously he tried to lynch Eddie to take suspicion away from himself — '

'We haven't forgotten Eddie,' Logan said grimly. 'You go to the house while I round up some men. No sense in getting involved in a shooting war.'

'No? You reckon I'll hang around while my restaurant is burnt down?' She wheeled the cow pony about and was away. She shouted back, 'Bishop will find out I can use a gun too!'

Logan swore; then a smile creased his face. It had been a long time since the boys got involved in a real fight. And Bishop's loggers were Yankees. He spurred his horse to a gallop, guessing that the boss would want to move fast.

There were more than twenty men on the big timber wagon as well as Bishop and Gregson with the driver when it started down the mud-rutted trail to Silver Gulch. Tough men with muscle and all armed. Men who wouldn't hesitate to kill for a hundred dollars.

The horses struggled to find a footing on the slope and kept sliding. Wagon wheels sank into the ruts. The driver complained, 'Too much weight, Mr Bishop. Best if some men walk alongside — otherwise we're goin' to get stuck fast.'

'Yeah,' Bishop said. 'That makes sense — okay, some of you drop off. Keep going, driver.'

It was still a slow descent even with some of the men walking. Tall pines and firs closed about them, lending a chill and dank air to the trail. Bishop was getting impatient and some of the loggers were losing their keenness. A hundred bucks was okay, but killing?

Bishop sensed their waning enthusiasm. 'An extra fifty bucks to the man who downs Farnsworth,' he called out. 'And another fifty to whoever brings Mary-Jane to me.'

Faces brightened as competition revived their enthusiasm. 'You bet, Mr Bishop.'

Beyond the trees the sun warmed and the wagon moved that bit quicker. Muddy boots began to step out. The derelict shacks at the edge of town showed, and men dropped off the wagon and spread out.

They unlimbered guns and began to move from one bit of cover to the next.

Bishop, with Gregson beside him, remained seated, taking the wagon down Main Street.

Ahead, in the middle of the road and facing them, a single figure showed, a man on a mare past her prime. It was the town marshal aboard Tildy, badge gleaming in the sunlight, shotgun lifting into a firing position.

# 17

'Stop right where you are,' Keyhoe called, shotgun levelled. 'You must hand over your weapons before coming into town.'

For one long moment when time seemed to stand still, he thought he might get away with it. Bishop's face went purple, then white, and he turned on Gregson, screaming, 'You — you stupid — you told me you killed him with a bomb! You — '

His outburst broke the spell.

Gregson ignored his boss. He took quick aim with a revolver, fired at Keyhoe and missed. He vaulted from the wagon and dived for cover. A bullet followed him, forcing him to keep his head down.

Bishop stood up in his seat, shouting, 'Get the dentist, kill him!' He loosed off a shot and jumped down and got behind the wagon.

A logger, running towards Tuttle's store, collapsed as a bullet struck him and he rolled off the boardwalk into the mud.

Keyhoe took advantage of the confusion and covering fire to wheel Tildy into the alley leading to the stable. He slid out of the saddle, climbed a ladder placed there to reach the roof and crouched behind the false front. He could hear Bishop screaming, 'Where are they? Where are the shots coming from? I can't see anybody!'

From a prone position Keyhoe watched Bishop's men scatter; the attack faltered as the loggers ran for cover. He raised his shotgun and triggered a barrel; pellets stung the wagon horses into motion and they pulled away down the street, removing a shield for the lumberjacks. Bishop, suddenly exposed, ran for his life.

Further along the row of false fronts, over Mary-Jane's restaurant, Sinclair used a rifle provided by the mayor. A logger cried a name, spun around and fell; the dude appeared to be a crack shot with a rifle too.

Bishop gave vent to a string of curses. Obviously he hadn't reckoned on any real resistance and only now realized the situation wasn't going the way he wanted. Keyhoe recalled Sinclair's words: 'He's practically frothing at the mouth,' and that was how he appeared as he shouted, 'Kill them — kill them all!'

Alice popped up above her baker's shop, fired, and ducked down again.

The timbermen finally caught on that the townsmen were on the rooftops and began to shoot back in earnest.

Keyhoe watched Farnsworth, with the big Sharps rifle, shooting down from the top of the Five Aces; the saloon owner seemed as cool as though he were dealing a pack of cards.

A heavy slug destroyed the shelter of one logger who went sprawling backwards.

Then the false front was swept by a

hail of lead; the upper structure was only thin wood and splinters filled the air.

Tuttle had warned them he had only a limited supply of ammunition and told them not to waste any. So far it seemed to be working; one shot at a time and change position.

Keyhoe saw the mayor drop another man from above his store, and wondered how long they could delay the end. There were a lot of tough *hombres* down there and they weren't short of ammunition. Without help the end was not in doubt; he hoped Mary-Jane would be able to get the cattlemen moving quickly.

He decided to try a different tactic and called, 'You men down there. It's Bishop and Gregson I want. If you leave quietly now the law will leave you alone.'

Bishop screamed in fury. 'Shoot him! Destroy him! Two hundred dollars to the man who silences him! Two hundred! Two . . . '

His voice was drowned out by a volley of shots going Keyhoe's way. Lead whined like an army of hornets on the warpath. Keyhoe flattened himself and crawled away across the roof.

Loggers were dodging from building to building, keeping under cover and snap-shooting as a target showed. One was careless and Keyhoe squeezed a trigger and gave him a barrel of shot.

A body jerked like a puppet and tumbled. Keyhoe withdrew to reload. Time was important; they had to buy time.

There was a temporary lull in the battle for Silver Gulch and he crawled to the edge of the roof, looking for Gregson; he had a score to settle with that one. The sun had gone and the sky was wintry-grey; a cold damp wind keened and he shivered.

Then he heard hoofbeats from the south. Mary-Jane was back, but she was alone. He shouted a warning.

He saw Sinclair shift position, and

Gregson wing a lucky shot upwards. Sinclair stumbled, grabbed for the edge of the roof and missed. He hit the boardwalk and rolled into the mud of Main Street and lay there unmoving.

Gregson edged closer to finish him off, grinning. A shot took his hat away and he darted back to cover, cursing.

A red light flared. Keyhoe glimpsed a flame from the corner of his eye; someone down there had lit a torch. Smoke billowed in the wind.

Hugo Bishop held a blazing torch aloft as he ran towards the saloon, screaming, 'Burn them out! Burn them to death!' The bright flame gusted as the wind caught it.

Crazy man, Keyhoe thought. Bishop seemed to have no fear, not realizing he had made himself a target. Perhaps he believed himself immortal at that moment.

One shot ended his dream.

The .50 slug from the buffalo gun in Farnsworth's hands took Bishop in the dead centre of his chest, lifted him off his feet and hurled him backwards into the mud. He fell on the torch, putting it out and obviously past feeling anything.

Alice dropped from her perch and ran into the street to straddle Sinclair, revolver in hand. Bullets flew past her but she stayed there, shooting back.

Gregson grabbed the reins of Mary-Jane's horse and dragged her from the saddle, using her as a shield.

Keyhoe half-climbed, half-fell down the ladder to get at him. He heard a drumming of hoofs and rebel yells as Cade's Texans came whooping down the street to the crackle of revolvers. Alice stood her ground and the riders split and surged past, chasing the loggers. The cowpunchers didn't seem inclined to take prisoners; it was the civil war all over again.

Keyhoe reached the street as Gregson dragged Mary-Jane towards North End, and he ran as fast as the mud would allow. Fighting still went on, but Cade's outfit would take care of that. It was the ghost he wanted.

The ex-miner was hauling her along the alley behind Main Street, heading towards the shack with the hidden mine shaft. No doubt he knew of another tunnel to aid his escape.

He handled her as if she were a sack of grain, even though she fought and struggled to free herself. He was immensely strong.

Keyhoe realized he wasn't going to be in time to stop Gregson reaching the shack, and shouted, 'Stand and fight, you coward — or can you only attack women?'

Gregson paused, looking back. He'd tried shooting this one, had left him to drown in a flooded tunnel, and tried a third time with an explosive. He scowled, almost tempted to turn on the man he hated most in the world. Almost, but not quite.

He needed an advantage before he faced Keyhoe.

Mary-Jane chose that moment of hesitation to viciously scrape the side of her boot down one of his shins. Gregson swore, pushed her aside, and staggered away.

'Run, Mary-Jane,' Keyhoe bawled. 'Get away and leave him to me!'

He charged at Gregson, eager to get to grips with him. Mary-Jane stepped back as Gregson drew a Bowie knife from his belt. He feinted as Keyhoe, grim-faced and threatening, came steadily at him; he dodged into the shack, the door swinging shut after him.

Keyhoe threw the shotgun to Mary-Jane. He kicked the door open and drew his truncheon. It was dark inside, and he paused.

After a few seconds his eyes adjusted and he became aware of a faint grey light coming in through dirty windows. There were shadows everywhere. He went in with a rush.

Gregson had been waiting for him. He laughed and slashed with the big knife. Keyhoe barely swerved sideways in time to avoid the blade. It was like fighting a knife held by a shadow — the door of the shack had swung shut again and the interior was a place of dark grey gloom.

Gregson struck again and this time Keyhoe parried with his truncheon; the lead inside it turned the blade.

Then Keyhoe lowered his head and charged like a bull that had been maddened beyond caution. He was furiously angry that this man had laid hands on Mary-Jane. He hit with all his weight and staggered him. Gregson gulped for air and lashed out wildly.

Wary of the open shaft somewhere in the shadows, Keyhoe was not quite quick enough and the steel slashed through coat and shirt to draw blood. He felt it trickle down his arm; immediately he closed the gap between them, taking the attack to the logger.

It was now almost too dark to see. He felt he was fighting a shadow that had come to life. He lost sight of his opponent as clouds gathered, making it even darker inside the shack. He groped for a wall to feel his way and thought he had nearly completed a circuit when his hand touched metal.

Keyhoe thought he'd met the keen edge of a knife but it was only a piece of metal sticking out from the wall; perhaps a support for a missing shelf.

He crouched low, waiting, straining to see in the darkness; he couldn't hear any movement and guessed that Gregson, too, waited for the first glimmer of light to return. Each second seemed to stretch to an hour.

Then a knife swished through the air above his head. Gregson mumbled an oath when he realized he'd misjudged his target, and tried to draw back.

Keyhoe smashed his truncheon into a kneecap.

Gregson shrieked in agony and stumbled backwards. Keyhoe rose and pursued him and used his truncheon on the knife hand. He heard the blade clatter on the floor and rushed in to finish the fight.

He remembered Mary-Jane and there was a lot of anger in him. He struck hard and deliberately, again and again; he heard a bone snap.

Gregson went further back, moaning, trying to avoid the punishing truncheon and, suddenly, he wasn't there any more.

Keyhoe barely managed to stop himself following Gregson down the shaft. He poised, swaying, on the edge of the drop, listening to a wailing scream, a sobbing and, finally, a dull thump; after that there was silence. Keyhoe stepped back a pace, shaking.

He stood still for long seconds, taking deep breaths, blood dripping from his arm. Then, satisfied that Gregson wouldn't scare anyone again, he moved towards the door.

Outside, Mary-Jane was waiting for him. The moon shone between clouds, turning her to silver. 'Come on, Phil — that arm needs washing and binding up.'

She took his good arm and led him

gently up Main Street towards her home.

★ ★ ★

The war was over. The Texans had returned to the Bar C and any surviving loggers were still running.

The celebration in the Five Aces was muted. Anson, the lawyer, had returned unexpectedly with news for Bishop, and that news spoiled the celebration. The powers-that-be, in Washington, had changed their minds and decided against the proposed railroad. It would now take an alternative route and the town would die.

'Bloody men,' Alice said, and held out her glass for a refill. Sinclair, in his role of bandaged hero, obliged her.

'All that killing for nothing,' Mary-Jane said sadly, holding Keyhoe's hand.

Tuttle added, 'So maybe I'll go to California after all.'

Only the dude was contemplating staying, undecided whether or not to take over the logging business.

'Actually, I like it here, but I'd have to hire new men from somewhere.'

'If you do,' Alice said with a hiccup, 'Maybe, just maybe, I'll keep you company!'

'Waal,' Wallace the coach driver drawled, 'if yuh can locate Rudge it would be a start. He ain't got far — we passed him coming here.'

They finished their meal and sat back, Keyhoe and Mary-Jane side by side contemplating their future. Farnsworth handed around another bottle.

The batwing doors parted and Virgil, dirty, unshaven and smelly walked into the saloon. He dumped his pack and surveyed the room. 'What's this? A party? Something happened?'

Farnsworth gave him a drink while the others took it in turns to explain the victory over Bishop and their defeat at the hands of those in Washington.

'Things happen sure enough,' Virgil agreed. 'But I'm real hungry, Mary-Jane.

Just got down from the far side of the gulch.'

'Wait here, Virgil, and I'll go rustle up a meal, and bring it to you.'

She went out and Virgil sat down next to Sinclair, who didn't even wrinkle his nose.

'Find anything?'

'Maybe, can't tell for sure till I get an assay. No vein, but I've seen stuff like this somewhere before.' The old prospector reached for his pack and rummaged through it. He brought out a canvas bag and spilled a handful of sand onto the table. It was black and looked heavy.

Sinclair showed an immediate interest and rubbed some of it between his fingers. 'Is there much of this?'

'Yeah, a helluva lot, practically a mountain, if it's worth anything.'

The dude smiled. 'It is.'

Mary-Jane returned with a platter and Virgil ate greedily. 'Looks like snow,' she said.

Tuttle's sharp gaze stayed on the

dude, who had a dreamy expression. 'D'yuh know anything about mining, Mr Sinclair?'

'I've told people before — ' he sounded a mite testy. ' — because I come from England and am paid to stay away doesn't mean I'm stupid. I've studied a bit of geology on my travels.'

'So what is it?' Keyhoe asked.

'This — ' Sinclair let the sand trickle between his fingers ' — is carbonate of lead — a compound of lead with silver and other minerals. At a guess it might separate out at forty ounces of silver to the ton.'

Tuttle said, 'So it looks like Silver Gulch is back in business.'

'And, this time, I mean to buy in right at the start.'

'Me, too,' Alice said.

Virgil pushed back his empty plate. 'Waal, then, let's celebrate all over again. Mr Farnsworth . . . '

Mary-Jane and Keyhoe exchanged smiles. He said, 'Looks like we can settle here after all. All we need now is a preacher.'

She looked through the window and saw the first snowflakes of winter. She leaned close and whispered, 'I don't feel like waiting for any preacher . . . and I've got a bear-skin rug in the back room, right next to the stove . . . '

## THE END

We do hope that you have enjoyed reading this large print book.

Did you know that all of our titles are available for purchase?

We publish a wide range of high quality large print books including:
**Romances, Mysteries, Classics**
**General Fiction**
**Non Fiction and Westerns**

Special interest titles available in large print are:
**The Little Oxford Dictionary**
**Music Book, Song Book**
**Hymn Book, Service Book**

Also available from us courtesy of Oxford University Press:
**Young Readers' Dictionary**
**(large print edition)**
**Young Readers' Thesaurus**
**(large print edition)**

For further information or a free brochure, please contact us at:
**Ulverscroft Large Print Books Ltd.,**
**The Green, Bradgate Road, Anstey,**
**Leicester, LE7 7FU, England.**
**Tel:** (00 44) **0116 236 4325**
**Fax:** (00 44) **0116 234 0205**

On the run from the law, Vince M'Cloud and his gang decided to take over the sleepy little town of Arrow's Flight and use it as their hideout. After killing the sheriff, M'Cloud instituted a tyrannical reign of gun law, holding the town under siege. Anger simmered amongst the populace, and plans of revenge were afoot. But it was the appearance of the mysterious outlaw Abe Fletcher that really threatened to turn events around . . .

# CAULDRON OF VIOLENCE

## E. C. Tubb

Young Colin Bowman, orphaned after an Indian attack, is left homeless and alone. But the Civil War beckons and Colin, fighting for the victorious Union army, finds adventure learning the art of war. After the conflict, Colin's adventures continue, guiding Sam Curtway and his daughter Julia's train safely through Indian country. Colin learns the value of love, and when Indians attack, lives hang in the balance. Now he must settle old scores and move on to a new life.

# LIGHTNING DRAW

## Hank Fisher

He drifted into the Golden Nugget saloon in the ugly township of Come Lucky . . . Born in a wild and six-gun-torn West — the Cougar Kid was named after the most vicious animal that roamed the country. He was an ordinary cowpoke, but lawlessness and savagery had turned him into a ruthless killer. And now men like Jumbo Jordan, a rattlesnake of a man who runs a protection racket, will find no mercy when they face the deadly Cougar Kid . . .

# THE LONESOME GUN

## Ken Brompton

It's a fateful day for Orde Clemmins, foreman of the Star and Bar Ranch. A mysterious stranger — the spitting image of Luke Strang — is driving cattle onto his land. But hadn't Clemmins and his men chased Strang to Skeleton Desert and certain death . . . ? In fact, Luke Strang's son, Rod has returned to Arizona to claim his inheritance. But the odds are heavily stacked against him — a bloody shoot-out means many men will die before justice is done.

# KILLER UNMASKED

## Sydney J. Bounds

When Big Jim Stead is shot dead in the back, it seems Cliff Brent is guilty. But he escapes the hanging and takes the owlhoot trail for four years. Returning to his hometown, he finds his first love, Mary, believes he's the killer. Worse still, she's engaged to Greg Halliday, owner of the Silver Horseshoe saloon. Cliff is determined to find Big Jim's killer — perhaps then he could win Mary's love. But would revenge and his gun-skills be enough?

# JUST BREATHIN' HATE

## Dempsey Clay

When the Law went loco and charged him with killing his wife, innocent Jack Fallon had two choices only — run or hang. So he ran — to a strange lost valley shut off from the world and ruled by a cult of holy men who would prove more lethal than any posse could ever be . . .